Bad Guy

by

Ana Diamond

Cover Art by *Tina Lynn Stout*

The Wild Rose Press, Inc.
PO Box 708
Adams Basin, NY 14410-0708
Visit us at www.thewildrosepress.com

Publishing History
First Edition, 2025
Trade Paperback ISBN 978-1-5092-6017-1
Digital ISBN 978-1-5092-6016-4

Published in the United States of America

Chapter One

"If they find out I'm a snitch, they'll kill me," Luke Daniels warned Special Agent Troy Wilson.

A hole-in-the-wall diner at a rest stop in northeastern Nevada was the last place Luke thought he'd ever find himself.

The agent's expression remained stoic. "That's a risk we're willing to take. It's you who needs to decide if walking free from cyber-crime and drug trafficking charges is worth it.

"Hmm. A max sentence of twenty years versus getting killed," Luke mused. "A lose-lose decision no matter what I decide."

Luke relaxed his posture while rubbing the stubble on his chin as the waitress set down two cups of black coffee in front of them; the roasted nutty smell instantly perked him up. She said nothing, barely acknowledged them with her heavily hooded eyes, as if she were doing her own hard time working at a diner until the end of her pathetic life. This dusty part of the world wasn't trying to please anyone.

As he glanced around the empty run-down diner, Luke knew he'd rather be here than in prison for most of his life. "Why me, Wilson? Why not find some guy who knows the mafia world?"

"If you're smart enough to run a massive drug ring, we're pretty confident you can infiltrate the Costa Crew.

We tend to select those who've had some success in their criminal lives. You raked in quite a bit of money during your stint, and you did it without losing any limbs. Resilience is the key to this game, which I believe you possess." He raised both palms in a "hold off" gesture. "Or you can spend the rest of your life in prison. It's your choice."

Luke's eyebrows shot up. "The Costa Crew has been operating like forever. No one gets in with them without having a blood relation or other long-standing connection. What makes you think I can?"

Hunching his shoulders, Wilson looked him straight in the eye. "Think of it as your biggest life-changing challenge. I wouldn't be sitting here if I didn't think you had a chance."

Luke sipped the bitter watered-down coffee as he studied the agent's dark, menacing eyes, slicked-back hair, and stocky build. His features were quite the contrast to Luke's light brown hair, green eyes, and lean frame. Troy Wilson made a much more convincing mobster than Luke Daniels.

"I don't even look the part."

"Even better. They'll see it as an asset since their rivals won't suspect you."

Defeated by the predicament he'd managed to get himself into, Luke slouched against the back of the ratty booth. What he was about to agree to would probably kill him—or worse—turn him into someone's slave for the rest of his life. But if he didn't agree to the plan, he'd be a slave to the prison system. For some people, being locked up might bring protection or peace.

For him, being incarcerated was much worse.

"What do I have to do?"

Troy broke his stone-faced expression with a slight smile. "We'll put you up in a small apartment in a town called Cliff's Edge, not too far from here. We have word that the boss of the Costa Crew may be hiding out there. We'll give you a little cash to live on, although it won't be much. There's a mom-and-pop grocery store not too far from here. The owner is looking for a part-time bagger."

Luke blinked hard. "Part-time bagger?"

"Yeah, you know, you place the groceries in the bags for the customers."

"I know what a bagger is. There wasn't anything else available?"

"Oh, what's the matter? You're too smart for the job."

Luke rolled his eyes.

"Don't get caught up in the small things," Wilson went on. "Your real job will be to get the Costa Crew comfortable enough to trust you, maybe even recruit you into their ranks."

Luke doubted that would ever happen. "They'll never go for it."

Troy's index finger shot up. "Almost impossible but not impossible."

"Will I wear a wire?"

"Eventually. We'll need to record them planning their next deal or murder."

Luke still wasn't convinced. "A wire is the first thing they'll look for."

"I didn't say it was going to be easy."

"Can I think about it?"

Troy nodded. "Sure. In prison. You can think about how you lost the opportunity for freedom."

Either way he could end up dead but human nature preferred freedom over being locked up like an animal.

And he was looking at a very long prison sentence.

"Fine. I'll do it."

****

"Sophia, when are you going to emerge from hiding and come out with us?" Tony Russo, her closest advisor, or consigliere, asked.

Standing in front of a mirror in the foyer of her house, Sophia Costa reapplied lipstick and smiled at her reflection. There was nothing better than a crimson velvet lip to lift her spirits. Ever since her brother Rocco was incarcerated on murder charges, leaving her to fill the role of boss of the Costa Crew, she had a lot going on.

"I agree, Tony. It's been a month since that order for a hit out on me and no one's made a move. If they think I'll hide forever, they've got another thing coming."

Tony flashed a set of white teeth that were quite a contrast to his tanned skin. "That's what I like to hear. Everyone's down at Lucky Guess for drinks. Take a load off, Soph, come have some fun."

Although she'd been diligent about staying out of sight for her own safety, having a drink with her people did sound appealing. "Maybe I will have one drink. Tell the driver I'll be out in a minute."

"Fantastic. I'll let everyone know the boss is coming. See you soon." Tony made his typical thumbs-up gesture and departed through the front door.

In reality, Sophia wasn't so thrilled. She'd been raised in the life of crime—it was all she knew. One month ago when her life had been threatened by a hired assassin, she thought about reconsidering her options—

not that she had much of a choice. After her brother went in for murder and was placed in solitary at a supermax out in Colorado, he appointed her the next boss. Keeping it in the family—so to speak—much to underboss Carmine Bruno's disapproval.

She took a moment to drag a brush through her long jet-black hair, adjust her gold collar necklace and made her way toward the car that idled out front. Maneuvering into the back seat wasn't easy in a tight black knee-length skirt and patent leather stilettos—but it'd been a while since she'd gone out and during the evening, April weather in this part of Nevada was breezy enough to send a chill down her spine.

"Good evening, Lorenzo," she said to her driver as she looked at him in the rearview mirror.

"Evening, Boss." He returned her glance with warm toffee-colored eyes and a full brow.

Sometimes, she realized, being a boss had its perks. "How's the family?"

"Good. Lucia is graduating high school in a month. She got a scholarship for college on the East Coast. We're so proud of her."

"That's amazing. Good for her to want an education and open her horizons."

Lord knows she hadn't had the same opportunities. In fact, before she'd been appointed boss, she'd been preparing to become someone's wife—a lifelong commitment to never knowing if your husband would come home alive—or tossed into the slammer.

"Yes, we want Lucia to have a different life with more options," Lorenzo said.

Secretly wishing she'd had the same advantage, Sophia had often imagined herself working at a major fashion house in New York City, as the boss, of course. "Bravo! Lorenzo."

"Thank you. Where to, Boss?"

"Lucky Guess."

"Right away. I haven't seen you go anywhere in quite some time. Are you celebrating something tonight?"

She smiled in the rearview mirror. "My freedom."

Chapter Two

Once officially enlisted to infiltrate the Costa Crew, Luke didn't exactly know where to begin. He figured approaching the lower-ranked members first might lead him to the upper levels. And if he knew anything about bad guys, they'd most likely hang out at neighborhood bars, bragging about their latest conquests.

Located far outside the Las Vegas strip, Lucky Guess was one of the bars he'd chosen to search for Costa Crew members. The other two places he'd hit over the past week were populated with elderly locals and not much else. On the other hand, the few times he went into Lucky Guess, he'd noticed a following of blue-collar workers looking for happy hour specials and quick bites at the bar.

Walking in with no weapons or wires on him, he had to prove to Troy he could get close enough to the Costa Crew to warrant further investigation. Until then, he was just a civilian getting a drink.

As he entered the nondescript establishment, he went straight to the bar, trying to appear as if this was his usual spot. Earlier, in his apartment, he'd practiced his background story. They'd just released him from prison for minor drug charges and he was looking to parlay his skills into a new venture. He believed he could use them to bring easy wealth. Plus, he wanted to be part of a tight-knit group of guys who look out for one another.

"What'll it be?" the bartender asked.

"Any IPA will do," Luke replied.

The bartender scrutinized him for a quick second, then set the opened bottle in front of Luke.

"Thanks. Cheers." He held up the bottle and took a drink, realizing he stuck out from the regulars and was likely being watched. But that was exactly what he wanted.

"My name is Martin," the bartender said. "I haven't seen you here before. Did you just move into town?"

Luke nodded. "Yup. My landlord said this was the place to be."

"Who said that? Chuck?"

Luke's eyebrows shot up. "Yeah, you know him?"

"I wouldn't say we're friends, but he owns a lot of the properties around here. He's also in here all the time. It's a wonder he's able to keep a job."

Luke chuckled, acutely aware he'd better watch what he said. "Small town."

"Very." Martin opened his eyes wide, then went over to serve more thirsty patrons.

It didn't take long for a young, stocky guy to sidle up to the bar next to Luke. "You lost?" he asked without looking directly at Luke.

"No, I'm staying in one of the Cliffside buildings on Cavern Road. I'm looking for some new business opportunities."

Young Guy sipped the brown liquid from his tumbler. "What kind of business opportunities?"

"One that will make everyone a lot of money."

Young Guy finally looked him in the eyes. Money— that got his attention. Luke noticed a yellowing bruise spread across his cheek and the long dark hair that constantly fell into his eyes. "Where'd you get the shiner?"

"Taking care of my brothers, as one should. What makes you think anyone will listen to you here?"

Luke shrugged. "You're listening. Aren't you?"

Young Guy smiled and stuck out a hand. "I'm Stefano. Everyone calls me Kid."

He grabbed and shook Kid's hand. "Luke."

"Where do you come from, Luke?"

"Prison."

Kid laughed and then poured the rest of his drink down his throat. He scrunched up his face as he swallowed. "Same."

An hour later, Kid's eyes were glazing over, his voice came out louder than necessary.

"You remind me of my friend Tony," Kid said, smiling wide. "He's also full of jokes."

Bingo! Troy had given Luke the names of the members of the Costa Crew and Tony Russo, as he remembered, was high in rank. Luke was pretty confident his new friend Kid was the ticket into the Costa Crew and he thought he'd positioned himself well enough to call it a night. He figured he could do this until Kid felt he could trust him enough to warrant an introduction to the higher-ups.

But right as Luke asked for the check, Kid's expression changed drastically, going from smiling ear to ear to a deer caught in headlights.

"Oh man, what's he doing here?" Kid said, looking around with help-me panic on his face.

At the entrance, a burly guy with a pug nose and dressed in a long black trench coat scanned the bar, like he was looking for someone. Kid turned toward the other end of the bar, signaling to a guy wearing a black fedora, who then promptly disappeared into the back room.

Pug Nose took notice of Kid's intervention and barreled toward him with gritted teeth. But before he could get his hands on Kid, Luke elbowed him right in the center of his face. He fell back, clutching his bloody nose, while Luke continued the onslaught until he sensed surrender. Then he jumped off him while the others in the crowd lifted Pug Nose off the floor. Blood ran down his face and soaked his shirt. The room fell quiet as the sound of stilettos clicking on the floor became louder by the second.

Luke shook off the pain in his knuckles as he watched the dark-haired beauty approach.

She stopped and stared at Pug Nose's injuries, quickly glanced at Luke, then back at Pug Nose. "Take this message back to your boss. We're not afraid of you and if you come back, we'll kill you one by one." She nodded at her crew to take Pug Nose away, then turned to Luke.

A nervous tickle made him clear his throat as she stared up at him with deep sapphire-colored eyes. He couldn't imagine what role she played in this dirty game full of thugs and thieves.

"I have to personally thank you for stepping in for Kid. What's your name, Fighter?" she asked with a tiny smirk on her full red lips.

"Luke Daniels. May I ask who you are?"

"My name is Sophia Costa. I'm the boss."

****

Earlier in the night, Sophia had entered Lucky Guess through the back door. Tony Russo, her closest advisor, greeted her with open arms. "Good, you came," he said, pecking her on each cheek. "The captains need to see you in person once in a while. It makes them feel like you care about the organization."

"I know. I know. You've been telling me that, but before Rocco went into solitary, he told me to stay out of sight. Not only is a hitman after me but the Esposito family wants me dead, too. If that happens, you know everyone in here will be dead."

Tony squeezed her arm. "You're under a lot of pressure. I understand. Take a seat over there by One Eye. I'll get you a drink."

She was lucky to have Tony. Over time, he'd become a father figure to her especially since her actual father had been murdered years ago. If she ever found out who killed him it would be their last day on this earth.

She made her way toward Sammy "One Eye" Morello's table.

"Sophia, how've you been?" he asked, his good eye scanning her face. He kept the other eye covered up with one of his many patches—he had quite a large collection.

No one except Sophia knew the true story of how he'd lost his eye. His own gun misfired during a gun battle, resulting in weapon shrapnel hitting his eye. Everyone else in the Costa Crew believed he'd been shot by rival member, Frankie Esposito, and survived to tell the tale. It was a secret and mutual bond Sophia and Sammy had shared since the incident. But due to her seclusion, she hadn't heard his gravelly voice in a while. In a way it brought her comfort. Sammy was one of the few members who would do anything for her.

"I'm hanging in there," she said. "Any problems with your crew?"

"I lost a couple guys in the scuffle over the pizza

joints. I could use some new recruits."

"I heard about that. You guys really fought hard to keep them. You should be commended." She sighed. "It seems we are constantly under attack."

"That means we must be doing something right if everyone wants what we have. You should feel proud."

"I guess that's one way to look at it. I wish I could enjoy it without the constant threat of being killed."

Sammy shook his head. "No such thing. I know your brother taught you combat skills, so I'm not too worried about your ability to protect yourself. It's all part of the job."

"Guess so." Looking around the room, she nodded toward the other captains sitting at a table against the wall. After she took over as boss, she'd been lucky not to have had defectors or traitors—except for one. Her eye caught the wrinkled stern face of Carmine Bruno, staring back at her.

Ever since Rocco appointed her the boss, Carmine remained sour on the decision even though he'd been given his own crew as a consolation prize. He'd been underboss for years and thought for sure he would be appointed boss and maybe that might've been the case but under the current set of circumstances, Rocco felt more comfortable appointing her the boss since she'd be the less obvious choice, leaving Carmine bitter to the core.

Holding two drinks in his hands, Tony finally returned and sat next to her. "Did I miss anything?"

"I see Carmine is in a good mood."

Tony chuckled. "His face is permanently stuck in that position. Don't let him get to you." He placed a vodka martini in front of Sophia and sipped his scotch on the rocks.

Sammy turned toward them. "You better be careful. Don't poke the bear."

"What's he going to do?" Tony shrugged. "He's old and soft. His crew is barely breaking even. Rocco knows we need more money coming in, but I think he hasn't whacked him because of the loyalty Carmine has shown him."

Sammy slapped the back of Tony's head. "Hey! Watch what you're saying out here. You're asking for a war. Carmine deserves better than that and Rocco knows he's been a team player despite the challenges. Leave Carmine alone and keep the peace."

"Geez, all right. I call it like I see it. He could use some pep in his step. That's all."

"Maybe he just needs a tan," Sammy said, pointing at Tony's face. "Maybe you should invite him to your tanning salon."

Tony howled with laughter. "You might be onto something."

Sophia shook her head at the two jokers, but she also knew Sammy had a point. Carmine Bruno was not someone to be messed with. Her only recourse was to let him be.

A wave of shouts could be heard coming from the front bar. Sophia thought nothing of it as bar brawls were fairly common, until the screams and sounds of furniture flying through air made it impossible to ignore. She turned to Tony. "What's that all about?"

Their lookout, Johnnie, came running into the back room. "Get ready! One of the Esposito soldiers is here."

The announcement caused every member of the Costa Crew to stand, drawing their weapon of choice in practiced moves. But as the commotion seemed to die down, Sophia rose. "All right, all right. I think it's over." She looked at Tony, who was putting his gun back in its shoulder holster. "Let's go see."

Chapter Three

Luke stared at Sophia. "You're the boss of the Costa Crew?"

"What's it to you?" Tony replied, keeping his hand on his gun in open view.

"It's all right, Tony." She smiled, clearly trying to lighten the tension. "It's not every day you see the boss in heels." Then she turned toward Luke. "Anyway, I need to thank you for stepping in when things got a little hairy."

"It's no problem at all," Luke said, struggling to keep the awe out of his voice. "In fact, I've been meaning to get a meeting with...the boss of the Costa Crew."

"She's very busy," Tony offered.

"It's all right, Tony," Sophia murmured. "It's the least I could do for someone willing to take on one of our rivals. We could go to my house nearby—"

"Over my dead body," Tony interjected.

Sophia sighed. "What location would be acceptable to you, Tony?"

"How about here?" His arms opened wide. "There are plenty of tables to choose from."

Luke understood why this Tony, who clearly was this woman's protector, didn't want him in her house. If they stayed here, they could keep an eye on him at the bar. "Fine with me."

Sophia picked a corner booth away from all the

chatter, but Luke knew with Sammy with the one eye and burly Tony around, he would not get her undivided attention. Her two guard dogs sat on opposite sides of their leader while Luke took a seat across from her.

"Best you're going to get, Fighter," Tony said.

"I'll take it," Luke replied.

"So, what is it you want to talk about?" Sophia asked.

Luke scanned the hardened faces staring back at him. Sophia seemed like the precious jewel they were protecting and while she likely had mobsters in her bloodline, he couldn't help noticing a touch of innocence. In one evening, he'd made significant progress. No doubt the Feds would agree to the next phase of the Costa Crew infiltration. "I wanted to propose a business venture."

"A business venture?" She nodded. "You wouldn't be the first. Go ahead."

"I know a lot about the drug industry. I have all the connections. I can run a business from A to Z and make everyone more money than you've ever seen before."

Sophia remained expressionless but the other two had raised their eyebrows at the sound of *more money*. Even if she wasn't on board, he believed, based on what Kid had let slip out of his mouth the first night they met, she could be convinced by her own handlers if only to make their money troubles go away.

"We don't usually work with drugs," Sammy said. "There's a lot of heat in that line of work."

Tony turned to Sammy, looked directly into his functioning eye. "But also, a lot of money."

Sammy cocked his head. "If there's one way to get the Feds to start paying close attention, it's by selling drugs."

Tony rubbed his chin. "I think what he's really saying is he wants to be part of the crew. Am I hearing that right, Fighter?"

"I can make those debts disappear," Luke said. "You don't need to know how I did it."

Sammy chuckled. "You can't be serious. You can't just come out of nowhere and become a member." Sammy turned toward the other two. "You hear this guy?"

"He's right," Tony replied. "At best, if Sophia agrees, we can work with you but what you're asking for would be impossible."

"All right, everyone calm down," Sophia interjected. "I want to talk to Luke alone."

The two handlers went silent. Luke perked up a bit. If he could get rid of those two, he might have a chance.

Reluctantly, Sammy and Tony left the table, but they didn't go far. They were still only a few feet away and they continuously watched him, hands on their respective guns, ready for anything.

"Don't mind them. They're just doing their jobs," Sophia said. "I'm not sure why they're so worried. You have an innocent look to you."

Luke almost blushed. He'd played to the usual stereotypes and expected to deal with a man. Now, he had to pivot and change his entire demeanor. He couldn't be sure, but Sophia did not seem like a ruthless killer. Even though his hands were sweaty, and his heart raced, he was not afraid of her.

"Where are you from, Luke?"

"North Ridge."

"Ah, just outside of the Las Vegas strip. You must

be familiar with how things work with us."

Luke nodded. His brain short-circuited as her spicy perfume wafted around him like a hungry python. "That's why I'm here. I think your group is set up well enough to launder any money I bring in, which would be in the millions."

She returned no facial expressions. "We can certainly consider working with you if you can guarantee to produce what you are claiming. However, you must know who you are dealing with here. My guys will show no mercy."

Her eyes pierced his soul like daggers. "Understood. I know who I am dealing with, and I can handle it," he said without blinking.

Then her expression softened. "I can have my guys set up a logistics and expectations meeting so that we're all on the same page."

She sounded more like a corporate manager than a mafia boss. He wondered if it settled better in her mind to think of this as a legitimate business. Her brother probably knew no one would suspect her of being the boss, thereby providing a cover. Smart move and perhaps a better scenario for Luke to get what he came for. "I am very grateful, but I want something more."

Sophia's sapphire eyes glittered as she straightened her spine and leaned slightly toward him. A slight smile formed as she seemed to process his words. For the first time since they sat down, she seemed interested. "What would you like?"

Luke swallowed hard. Losing focus now in the face of beauty would be foolish of him. This was his chance. He had her undivided attention.

Don't blow it.

"I want in."

****

Sophia's shoulders slumped. His request wouldn't be possible. When was the last time the Costa Crew took anyone in who wasn't part of the family? As the boss, she held supreme power over decisions affecting the organization, but she had to carefully consider how everyone else would react. "If you've done your research, you already know how difficult it is to become a member, even when you're part of the family."

He nodded. "I know the rules but as far as I'm concerned, rules are meant to be broken. You need some fresh blood and I think I would be valuable to your group. I have all the connections for a quick and easy start-up. I bring both brains and brawn."

Sophia blinked away her inappropriate thoughts. Of course she'd noticed. His tall lean frame and fair complexion was different from what had been around her most of her life. And she wouldn't call him a tough guy either. He represented something new and refreshing. He reminded her of another life, of the freedom she'd been craving.

She wanted to learn more about the stranger who dropped out of the sky and right into her lap. "Right, you've said you'd be important to us. Tell me more. You probably already know everyone in the crew has grown up in this life and accepts all the issues that come with it but what got you into the life of crime?"

One corner of his mouth lifted. "Growing up, I was really good at computers. In fact, I'd planned on going to college for a degree in computers, but we fell on hard times, and I ended up getting a job in a repair shop, fixing up motorcycles and thinking maybe I could save up and enroll in a program at some point."

She nodded. "That makes sense."

"But that's not what happened."

"That's too bad. Your talents were wasted."

He returned a sheepish grin. "I met some guys at the bike shop who took me to a makeshift lab. Needless to say, they weren't making blood pressure medicine there. I knew I'd be getting myself in some real trouble if I got caught but once they showed me the stacks of cash they'd stashed above the ceiling panels, there was no stopping me. I justified it in my mind as money I could send back to my family and an easier way to rake in the coins than going to college."

"Once you get used to that kind of money it changes people."

"In the worst ways. Once I got a taste of the street business, I went off on my own, distributing and selling drugs online. My business blew up and the rest is history. What about you? How'd *you* end up being the boss? Seems a bit out of character for the mob."

Her eyebrows shot up at him as she sipped her cocktail. "Because I'm a woman?"

He put his hands up in defense, triggering dirty looks from Tony and Sam. "Sorry, I meant no offense. This kind of organization tends to be no-girls-allowed even if you are perfectly capable, which I'm sure you are."

Sophia felt herself soften toward him. "That's true, it's not normal practice." The ease with which he shared his life story made her want to open up her otherwise tightly controlled world to him—even against her crew's advice. "My brother, Rocco, was the boss, but he's been locked up in a supermax, so he decided I should take over. It makes the crew feel confident about the stability of the organization." She clinked the martini glass with her long red nails. "I'm sorry I'm venting all my problems to you. I probably shouldn't be telling you this stuff."

"Don't be sorry. It sounds like you've been put in a tough spot. With all due respect, you don't sound too thrilled about it."

She fidgeted with the overfilled olive pick, feeling a bit exposed. He was right. She wasn't thrilled at all, but she hadn't realized he could see right through her big boss persona. "The truth is, before my brother went to prison, I was being pressured to marry and run a household with my eyes shut to reality. Each day my husband would come home for dinner from who knows where and I would not be able to ask any questions about it."

Luke nodded. "That would be hard."

"My routine would be filled with uncertainty and a duty to remain strong and loyal. At one time I saw myself moving to New York, maybe getting a job in fashion. Running around a bunch of hooligans with the threat of jail time at any moment was not on my to-do list." She noticed his mood darkened. "Most of these guys have done some time, but I'd like to avoid it if possible." She shrugged her shoulders. "I'm not exactly sure how that would work."

"That's why you need me." He leaned in, capturing her attention. "I know what the Feds are looking for and how to avoid getting on their radar. I've learned that the Costa Crew owns multiple pizza joints where we can launder the money I make for the organization. It will all go smoothly. I promise."

His intense stare turned her stomach into knots. She glanced at Sammy and Tony who still patiently watched them. This guy seemed different. He didn't give the usual spiel about how much he loved the Costa Crew and wanted nothing more than to be part of it. Normally, an outsider soliciting her would be a red flag in the organization. You wanted new recruits to be familiar and trustworthy, therefore you don't take chances.

But she was tired of following the tradition. She was in charge now and maybe it was time for a change. "We may have recently had a spot open up for a new recruit."

His smile widened.

She signaled for her crew to come back to the table. "Looks like Fighter here may have convinced me to let him be a candidate."

Sammy threw his hands up. "You can't be serious? We can't take this kind of heat."

Sophia's stuck her chin out. "I'm dead serious."

"All right. Let's calm down," Tony said. "I'm not that worried. He probably won't make it past the tests anyway."

"Tests?" Luke asked.

Tony leaned close. "You heard right. There will definitely be tests."

Chapter Four

"You've done good."

Special Agent Wilson used a small spoon to stir the cream in his late-night coffee. "I have to say I'm amazed. At best I thought you'd overhear something interesting, but to actually meet the boss and possibly get recruited as a member?" He slapped the table. "You've got some skills, Daniels. I think everyone back at the office would agree that we can proceed to the next phase."

Luke was surprised. Things were moving quickly; he'd barely had time to process the last twenty-four hours. "Next phase? Which is what?"

"We send you off with a wire. If we can't get it on tape, we can't build a case."

He should have been thrilled with his progress, but he hadn't been prepared for Sophia Costa. "Right, but you failed to mention a couple details."

"Such as?"

Luke leaned forward in his booth seat. The minestrone soup he'd ordered shook as his chest bumped the table. He whispered even though there were no other customers around to hear them. "Such as, the boss is a woman?"

"I might have left that out when I gave you some of the more important crew member's names. I didn't want to spook you so early on." Troy looked down at his coffee. "We've been tracking her for years. She's kept a low profile. Her brother was the boss but since he's been doing prison time, he passed the baton to her. She's got a backbone, but I doubt she's the grim reaper."

Luke's eyes narrowed. "What does that mean?"

"It makes no difference if the boss is a man or a woman as long as you get the recordings I need to convict."

"It makes a difference to me." Luke pointed to his chest. "Maybe I'm not as cold-hearted as you think. What role has she actually played? It seems to me she was forced in by her brother without a say in the matter."

Troy leaned back in his seat, smiling. "Wow, you really got the scoop quickly. How did you manage to charm all her secrets out of her?"

Luke pursed his lips. "I think she's looking for something else in her life. I happened to come in at the right time and what I told her was exactly what she wanted to hear. From what she told me, she is not a cold-blooded killer."

"All right, you need proof on her?" Troy pulled a phone out of his inner jacket pocket and began tapping on the screen. He then handed the phone to Luke. "This is a report on some of our intel on Sophia Costa."

Luke scanned the document.

Undercover surveillance observed Sammy Morello, a known Costa Crew captain, leaving the home of mob boss Sophia Costa on the evening of February sixth. He arrived at the Deluca home at 0100 hours and wasn't seen again until he left their home one hour later. He then returned to his residence. One week later a neighbor reported to law enforcement that the entire family hadn't been seen for several days.

"This doesn't mean much to me." Luke frowned.

"Who knows what happened to them?"

"I'll tell you what happened to them." Troy's voice came out stern. "When the cops entered the home they found the whole family dead. She sanctioned the murder of a family who refused to pay off their loans. It was done to set an example to anyone else thinking they could get away with not paying."

"The entire family?"

"That's right. Even the teenagers since they were also involved. As far as I'm concerned, she's just as evil as her male counterparts, and I've made it my personal mission to eradicate these types from the earth." He jabbed his pointer finger into the table and leaned in toward Luke. "Between you and me, ever since my field partner got killed by one of the Costa Crew, I have even more of a reason to bring these guys down."

Luke handed the phone back to Troy, shaking his head in disbelief. "I'm sorry about your partner but I'm sure there's a good explanation for the deaths of the teenagers."

He couldn't imagine Sophia could be that cruel. Or maybe her hand had been forced in the matter. Regardless, he'd be sure to ask her about it at some point.

"A good explanation?" Troy's voice rose as he crossed his arms over his chest. "I guess you'll be finding out the hard way how these people operate. Is there a reason you are defending the boss of a highly organized illegal operation that has resulted in hundreds being killed?"

Luke could barely make eye contact. "What are you talking about?"

"Could it be that you're smitten with her?"

"Look, it changes things—"

"It shouldn't. We're still dealing with criminals. She's a participant in this even if she's not pulling the trigger. But if you're feeling sorry for her and can't fulfill your duties, I'll pull you off the case now. We need someone we can trust to get the job done without hesitation and you seem to have a good handle on how to get through to them. But it's your choice."

Luke swallowed. Sophia Costa was the unexpected hitch in the plan. Despite what the report had said, he was sure she was no killer but rather an unfortunate product of her environment—a pawn in a game she wanted no part of. How would he mentally reconcile her ultimate demise if he were to proceed with the plan? He had yet to figure it out. "You also didn't tell me about the tests."

"Tests? What tests?"

"You want me to become a new recruit in the Costa Crew—that won't be so easy. They didn't go into detail, but I assume I'm going to have to prove myself worthy— maybe jog a few laps and get them drinks for a while?"

Troy nodded. "Yeah, it'll be some of that and much worse."

"Great."

"You seem to be a quick study. I don't think it will take long to catch on and when you do become a member, you'll have the trust and access we need to get proof on record." Troy smirked. "Unless you can think of another way to get to the top?"

Luke frowned. "Are you kidding me?" His voice came out raised. "What do you take me for?"

Troy put his hands out in surrender. "All right, take it easy. Anyway, it looks like you already have the boss's ear. The rest will come with time."

"I may be a criminal, but I do have my limits."

"Understood. And even if they rake you over the coals for a bit, it's a small price to pay for freedom. Wouldn't you agree?"

Luke stared down into his untouched soup. He doubted it would taste any good in this run-down diner and he'd lost his appetite anyway. Things were getting complicated faster than he'd expected. So far, he'd met a beautiful mob boss he believed to be innocent but was helping send to prison for the rest of her life and over the next few days he'd be performing humiliating tasks while in deep sleep deprivation—it sounded amazing.

Troy repeatedly tapped his hand on the stained off-white laminate countertop. "I never tell informants this, but I really feel that you have a talent in this line of work. I'm confident you're going to make it all the way. If you stick to the plan I see a happy ending here for you. So? What do you say? Ready to jump in?"

Luke shrugged. "The water is starting to look a little murky but what choice do I have?"

Troy shook his head. "That'd be less than none."

****

Over the last few days, Sophia's mood brightened. No longer stuck inside her house like a recluse, she wanted to witness Luke's rise through the ranks. Traditionally, her captains would take over the role of hazing, but she wanted to see for herself what he had to offer on his first day with the crew. Fighting through yawn after yawn, she waited past midnight for Luke to enter Lucky Guess and when he finally did, Sammy pounced.

"Fighter, drop and give me twenty!"

The rest of Sammy's crew cheered as Luke went straight to the floor and pounded out twenty push-ups without stopping. Then he rose up, barely fatigued.

"How about another twenty?" Sammy announced to the crowd.

More cheering ensued.

Luke went down again without complaint and pumped out another twenty. This time rising up a little slower.

"Another twenty?" Sammy asked the crowd.

His crew screamed for more blood as Luke went down to the ground slower this time.

"Ah, but wait," Sammy announced. "Let's make this more fun." He pointed to Kid. "Sit on his back."

Kid and the rest began laughing as he slammed his body onto Luke's back, pushing him face down into the ground.

"He's had enough!" Sophia announced as she pushed through toward Luke. The click of her heels could be heard in the abrupt silence.

After Kid scrambled off Luke's back, she leaned over, making eye contact with Luke. "Get me a drink, Fighter."

He nodded, rising off the floor to approach the bar obediently while the rest of the crew went back to minding their business. Sammy took a long sip of his scotch while keeping his good eye on Luke.

She moved to stand next to Luke at the bar, tapping her foot without a clue of her next move. She'd been part of the new recruit hazing process before and had no issues doling out commands if needed, but this felt different. He'd been an open book with her so far, which was highly unusual for those who had joined in the past. Usually, new recruits felt the need to pump themselves up to appear more capable than they actually were. By the end of the hazing process, it became very clear who was worthy. As the boss, she needed to show interest and be somewhat involved but in Luke's case, she had no interest in watching the boys torture him.

"Hang in there with the menial tasks," she told him. "The crew will want to run you around for a bit to gain their trust and build a partnership."

Luke laughed. "You sound like a human resources exec. Don't worry, I had an older brother growing up, so this isn't so bad. In fact"—he shrugged—"it feels natural."

Sophia grinned as she took a sip of her martini. "Thanks for the drink." She placed the glass back on the bar—gingerly to prevent spillage. "I think you give off an innocence that I'm trying to protect. Most recruits are brutes and sometimes torturing them for being the creeps they are, is a pleasure for me. If I told you how many of them behaved inappropriately toward me, you'd be horrified. That's why I wear stilettos." She lifted her leg up behind her, demonstrating her footwear disguised as weapons. "Slamming a heel into their skulls wouldn't even phase me in the least."

He leaned back, glancing at her shoe. "I see. That sounds brutal." Then he leaned toward her. "I'll let you in on a little secret."

"What's that?"

"The truth is, I have no pride."

"I somehow doubt that."

He leaned even closer to her. "It's true. You can do whatever you want to me. I won't take it personally or retaliate. So don't worry about saving me from the onslaught. I can take it."

His confidence was impressive to her. "I'll keep that

in mind, but you might want to save some energy. The last guy who wanted to be in the group didn't make it."

His eyebrows shot up. "Really? How'd it go down?"

"They made him bungee jump off the tallest building on the Las Vegas strip. They did it because they knew he was afraid of heights."

"Animals."

"I remember seeing his legs shaking at the edge of the platform and I'll never forget his blood-curdling scream as he dropped. The bungee cord bounced him back up safely, but he never came back to resume his hazing the following day."

"Understandable. That's a bit extreme. If it were me, I might do the same. I never liked heights either."

"Well, no worries. Sammy and Tony seem to like you enough not to go that far, I think, but I should still keep an eye on them."

His megawatt smile shook her to the core. "You're too kind."

"Hey, Fighter." Tony walked up to the bar, slapping Luke in the back. "Go wash my car out front. The kitchen said they've got some towels you can use. It's a black sedan."

"Sure thing," Luke said without complaint. He walked out the front like an obedient animal.

"Really, Tony? You couldn't think of anything less humiliating?" Sophia asked.

Tony shrugged. "Why should it be less painful for him? All the others had to go through this too. Listen, I'm doing you a favor. If he's not doing the grunt work, the rest of the guys are going to think you're letting him off easy. They're going to think you have a thing for him and then they're going to get pissed off at how you're treating him differently."

Sophia glared at Tony.

"Well, it's true. That's the last thing you want them to think. You'll lose all kinds of credibility. I'm just looking out for you. That's my job."

She swallowed her pride, knowing she had more to worry about than her feelings. "You're right, Tony. Thanks."

"Anytime." He left her there at the bar to go supervise Luke's progress with his car.

She sipped her cocktail, enjoying the burn down her throat. Tony was right. She was letting the others see the effect Luke had on her. She'd been dazzled by this departure from the usual routine, and she'd welcomed the change with open arms. It didn't help that he was also easy on the eyes, to the point where she was acting out of character and unable to stop herself. She threw down the rest of her drink, trying to quiet her negativity. The real question was, did she care enough to go back into hiding and repress her feelings? She already knew the answer.

Chapter Five

The hairs on Luke's neck stood to full attention as he sat in between Sammy and Tony in the backseat of Kid's SUV with a trailer hooked up to the back. Until now he'd mostly been tasked with being everyone's assistant or runner, but when Sammy called and said they were going to teach the Esposito family a lesson, he sensed this was serious.

"If Frankie Esposito thinks he can send over one of his goons to Lucky Guess to rough up our guys and not pay the price, he's got another think coming." Sammy sneered.

"Where exactly are we going?" Luke asked.

Sammy turned to look at him. "What's the matter? Are you nervous or something?"

Luke avoided Sammy's good eye. Clearly, he'd overstepped by asking the question.

"Don't worry, Fighter. It's nothing but fun and games around here."

Luke wasn't crazy about being driven somewhere unknown for who knows how long with no time to plan his escape. But he wasn't going to let them know he was sweating it either.

"All right, well, wake me up when we get there." He slid his body down in the seat, crossed his arms and shut his eyes. Truthfully, he could use a little sleep after all the errands he'd been running.

"Sweet dreams, Fighter," Sammy said in a creepy voice.

But Luke didn't react. After all, that's what they wanted, to scare him away and prove to Sophia that he didn't have what it took to be a member of the Costa Crew. They had another think coming to them.

After enough time passed for Luke to fall dead asleep, a pothole in the road jolted his head up. He looked around at his dim surroundings. "Where are we?"

"We've almost arrived at the Esposito farm," Tony said, taking a swig from his flask.

Luke nodded as he sat up in the seat, trying to shake off his exhaustion.

"I hope you slept well because we are going to steal their Thoroughbred horse and sell it to the racetracks," Tony explained.

"Correction," Sammy said, turning his good eye toward Luke. "*You're* going to steal the horse."

"*Me?*" Luke pointed to his chest. "I don't even know how to ride a horse."

"No one said to ride the horse," Sammy replied, "although if it comes to that, you'll be fine, just don't panic."

"Do either of you know how to ride a horse?" Luke asked.

Tony straightened his blue silk tie. "We look like farmers to you?"

Kid slowed the car on the highway, preparing to make a left turn down a barely lit dirt road. By the time they'd arrived at the Esposito place, the starless sky had darkened to almost complete blackness. No one would find his body here, not in a million years. The Feds would lose their informant, but they would get to listen to the recording of the gruesome events that occurred here.

"Pull over behind that tree," Sammy said. "Tony will be the lookout; Kid stays in the car, and Luke goes with me to the stables. The main house is down that road, a few minutes' walk from here. Tony will make sure no one is coming from that direction, while we head over to the stables. Everyone on foot should put shoe covers on." He pulled some out of his jacket pocket and handed them out to Luke and Tony. "All right, let's get going."

Luke took long quick strides alongside Sammy under the veil of darkness on the dirt road leading to the stables. "Isn't stealing their horse going to make them madder?"

"We're going to make it look like the horse got out and ran away," Sammy explained. "Happens all the time. These prize horses can be unpredictable sometimes and the Esposito crew probably stole them from somewhere anyway, so I bet the horses would try to run away if given the chance. We're basically giving one of them freedom. Here, put these gloves on."

"I guess that's one way to look at it," Luke said, slipping on the gloves.

He followed Sammy around to the side of the structure where the horses would be let out to the pasture. The pungent smell of manure stung his nose, and he heard the horses snickering as they approached—no doubt they knew someone was coming.

Sammy led the way as they approached the first stall. He peered through the stall grates. "This one will do." He read the name on the door. "Colonel Steed."

Luke also took a look inside. A horse with a shiny dark brown coat stood in the center of the stall, its tail swishing side to side.

"We need a rope to tie around his neck," Sammy said, looking around for something suitable.

"You mean a bridle?" Luke said.

Sammy stopped in his tracks. "You said you had no idea about horses. You sound like you've done this before. Do you see one of those lying around?"

"Here's one." Luke grabbed the dark brown leather ropes from a hook near the stall.

"Watch the horse crap." Sammy pointed to the brown pile Luke almost stepped on. Sammy studied the rope, looking a bit unsure. "It's probably pretty straight forward. You slide that over the horse's snout."

Luke's forehead wrinkled. "Snout? I don't think that's what it's called."

"All right, genius. Let's keep it moving. You seem to have this under control. I'll meet you down the road. Don't take too long."

Luke watched Sammy walk away, leaving him with a nine-hundred-pound animal and a skinny rope to lead it. "Is this part of the hazing?"

"Just do it," Sammy half-whispered, half-yelled.

"Awesome," Luke muttered to himself. He could see the horse's large eyes—the size of bread plates—following his every move through the door grates. "All right, Mr. Steed. You get to leave this place. So, any cooperation would be greatly appreciated."

Again, the horse swished its long brown tail.

"I guess it's now or never."

Luke opened the door latch, while holding the bridle up in his right hand as if to show the horse what his intentions were. He took a step toward the horse, now noticing the muscular tendons in its legs and well-groomed coat of hair. "It's all right. I'm not going to hurt you," he said as he lifted the bridle toward the horse's muzzle.

But as he took another step, the horse reared up and neighed in fear. Luke stepped out of the way to avoid getting trampled. In doing so, the horse made a run for it. Before the animal could get away, Luke reached out with the bridle in front of its face, causing the horse to slow up while he threaded the rope past its ears. Once the bridle was on, the horse stopped in its tracks, allowing him to buckle the straps under its chin. "There we go. That's not so bad. We're just going for a little walk." He slowly walked ahead of the horse, leading it forward with the reins.

"Ah, Fighter," Sammy said, walking back into the stable. "Look at you. You're a natural."

Luke wanted to tell him he was a jerk for letting him almost get trampled while he stood around nearby, pretending to be doing something useful. But as the lowly runner, he didn't have that kind of relationship with Sammy yet.

The horse cooperated for the most part as they walked onto the road leading back to the car. Until a light shined on them from behind. They both turned around toward the headlights beaming at them.

"Oh, man!" Sammy yelled. "It's a car coming from a different entrance. Let's go. Get on that horse."

Luke leaped onto the horse, pulling the reins over its head. Sammy jumped on behind him. He'd never ridden a horse before, but he'd seen riders signal the horse with their calves to move. Not wanting the horse to rear up, he gently tapped the horse's rib cage with his legs. Colonel Steed jolted forward from the slight pressure

Luke had applied.

Sammy leaned back in response, almost falling off. "Whoa! Go faster. We've got a move."

The horse galloped down the road like a true racehorse. With each step, Luke's body rose up and then crunched back down on the horse's bareback. If he made it out alive tonight, he will be feeling the pain tomorrow. Up ahead they could see the trailer with its back doors open wide, waiting for their arrival. Tony stood near it, ready to shut them after the horse went inside.

When they got close enough, Luke pulled on the reins to slow the horse but this time it reared up, throwing them off its back. Luke's body slammed to the ground and rolled away, the impact knocking the breath out of him.

Miraculously, nothing on his body felt broken as he lay on his back listening to Tony coax the animal into the trailer.

"Fighter, you all right?" Sammy said, coming up to his side.

"Yeah, I'm all right. You?"

"I bounced right back up like a jack rabbit," Sammy said. "I tell you, it's all that scotch I drink."

"Yeah, I bet that's what it is," Luke said.

"Come on, we need to go," Kid yelled from the car.

As Luke forced himself off the ground, his muscles protested that particular decision. But if a car was coming, they'd better move.

Tony had locked up the horse and jumped into the car with Kid in the driver's seat. Luke raced to the car with Sammy on his heels. They leaped inside as Kid stepped on the gas.

Looking behind him for the threat, Luke saw no

headlights flashing at them. "Where'd they go?"

"Looks like it was a false alarm," Sammy said. "The car must've turned. It went a different way."

Luke started breathing again. "False alarm?"

"Yeah, good thing too," Sammy said. "You moved a lot faster when you thought they were coming for us." His shoulders rocked as he laughed. "Right, Tony?"

"He sure did move fast, almost got trampled by the horse too," Tony chimed in, offering Luke his flask.

Kid snickered from the driver's seat. "He moved faster than lightning."

"What a valiant effort, Fighter," Sammy added. "We got the horse. Everyone's mostly all right. I couldn't ask for a better heist. Wouldn't you say?"

Luke snatched the flask from Tony, downing whatever was left inside. Then he wiped his mouth. "I hate you guys."

Chapter Six

"You look like crap," Troy Wilson said, staring across from Luke in their usual booth. The twenty-four-hour diner they'd chosen for their meetups had little to no patrons, which allowed for their private meetings at the crack of dawn.

"I've been busy," Luke replied, slumped in the booth. Greasy strands of hair fell over his eyes. The crew had him running around so much lately, he hadn't had time to wash his hair in days.

"They've got you doing the scut work, huh?"

"All night, every night and I started working at that god-forsaken grocery store you've graciously set me up with."

Agent Troy Wilson raised his hands in defense. "How much better could I do with an ex-convict as my applicant pool? Larry, the owner, has been nothing but gracious in letting you work there, and I purposely picked something that wasn't too taxing since I wanted all your attention to be focused on this mission."

Luke raked his hand through his hair, the grease acting like a gel. "You are too kind. Larry tiptoes around me like at any moment I'm going to pull out a bazooka and mow everyone down."

"I call that power."

"I call it insane. You should know how things are going, you've got the recordings."

Troy sniffed before swallowing more of his coffee. He did a quick visual search, looking for anyone that could be listening. But at this time of the morning, the diner was virtually empty. "Yeah, about those recordings, the horse heist was interesting, to say the least. That's definitely a crime. It's not quite what I was looking for but at least it's something. You think you could retrace their steps to the Esposito farm?"

Luke shook his head. "It was dark as pitch, and I had no idea where we were going."

Troy looked him up and down. "That's a shame. We've been trying to locate that farm for years."

"You guys couldn't think to put a locator on the recording device? This is the FBI, is it not?"

"Sounded like you fell off that horse." Troy ignored his question. "Did you break anything?"

"I don't think so, but my spleen hurts," Luke said, grabbing his right flank.

"Spleen? I'm no doctor but I don't think that's where your spleen is. You should probably get that checked out."

Luke's eyes narrowed. "Don't act like you care what happens to me." He took the recording device out of his jeans pocket. "All you care about is this." He slapped it on the table.

Troy crossed his arms and breathed in. "It's a start but it's not enough."

Luke groaned and let sarcasm ooze. "Of course not."

"Look, I know it's been hard lately, but I've also heard a lot of flirting mixed in with talk about professional boxing matches. That's not going to cut it."

Luke's right eyebrow arched. "There's no flirting. I have to get *everyone* to like me."

"Sure, you do. But the longer you're flirting instead of digging for incriminating information, the longer this is going to take. And those dark circles are telling me you're not up for it."

"I'm fine." Luke gulped down the rest of his black coffee. "I think I'm close to being invited to help out on a real job, a collection from clients that owe money. That'll probably be more relevant. Up until now, they've been testing my loyalty but I'm sure the real test is coming."

Troy rubbed his chin. "That does sound promising. If things go sour, there could be some bloodshed. I hope you're right for your own benefit. The sooner we get the information, the sooner we rid the world of mobsters and the sooner I can pull you out."

Luke smiled. "Again, don't act like you actually care what happens to me. Any one of them at any moment could blow my head off without blinking twice."

"That's the price of freedom."

Luke slammed his hands on the table, causing his almost empty coffee cup to jump up from its saucer. "Don't you think I know that? You think I'm doing this for fun?"

Troy leaned in. "On the contrary, from what I know about you, a little danger never bothered you. In fact, you can't seem to get away from it." He pulled out a worn folder from the brown leather bag next to him. Rifling through the stack of papers inside, he finally stopped searching toward the bottom of the stack. "Ah, here's the list. Trespassing—"

"I just wanted to see if I could scale the building with no harness." Luke shrugged. "It's just mountain climbing in an urban setting."

"Speeding and reckless driving—"

"I was told the car could go really fast and I was testing it out on an empty street. The only person in danger was me. These are all barely crimes."

"I doubt a judge will see it that way. The point is you like to test the limits and breaking the law is not a hard stop for you."

Luke leaned back in his seat, staring at the ground. His mind flashed to the day the Feds rushed into his inconspicuous apartment out of which he'd been running his entire million-dollar business from his computer.

Eight guns pointed at his head as they shouted commands he barely understood. With his face pushed into the rug, everything moved in slow motion as they confiscated all his files and electronics. And while his arms were pulled back behind him in a painfully unnatural position, he remembered realizing it was all over. The risky behavior, all the lies he told anyone he loved, and he recalled a sense of calming relief flooding over him.

He couldn't be that much of a masochist to want to go back there again and even though he'd done a lot of bad things in his life, he wanted to believe he wasn't truly a bad guy. "Have you ever considered that maybe I've changed? Maybe I want to change."

"Change? You can't change. People who do bad things are addicted to the rush. There's science behind that statement. Trust me."

Luke glared at Troy. "I think you're wrong. I've left all that behind me and now I'm trying to start over—a new life."

Troy got up, throwing a few dollars on the table to

pay the bill. "It's not the first time I've heard that. Now get me something I can use for this case and get some rest."

****

Sophia's fingertips prickled right before she went out for a collection with her crew—not from fear, but more like her nerves were on high alert. And since she'd been hiding out from the hitman for quite some time, it had been a while since she joined her crew to collect on money owed to them. This time they were paying a visit to Joe Manero. Known to her crew as "The Gambler," Joe owed them a lot of money and because he stopped returning their phone calls, the only way to get it back was by force.

Sophia sat sandwiched between Sammy and Luke in Kid's SUV as he drove to Joe's house. Sammy brought the big guns, Luke had his fists, and Sophia brought her level-headedness—which all combined, she thought, made for an effective team. The cool desert night made goose bumps form on her skin, but almost as soon as they appeared, they faded by the heat emanating from Luke and Sammy.

"He's home," Kid said after pulling over near the house but far enough away to remain hidden. "I can see the TV is on in the living room."

"Of course he's home," Sammy spat. "You think I'd come all this way into the desert for nothing? This is your chance, Fighter. To prove to us you've got what it takes."

Luke nodded. "Is there a plan? Do I get a weapon?"

Sammy leaned forward to get a better view of Luke on the other side of Sophia. "The plan is we go in there and do whatever is necessary to get our money back. *Capisce*?"

Luke said nothing in return.

"I've got what it takes. Let me lead this collection," Kid said. "It's the only way you're ever going to see that I should be made a member."

"Nah, not this time, Kid."

"You always say that."

"You've got a long way to go and a lot more to prove before we'll let you lead a collection run. Now let's go before they decide to leave the house and then there will be bloodshed in the front yard for everyone in the neighborhood to see," Sammy said.

Kid cursed and got out of the car.

"I'll go first," Sammy ordered. "Luke will follow behind me. Everyone else stays back until we secure the place."

Dressed down in jeans and sneakers for combat, Sophia recalled the fight moves Rocco had taught her when they were younger. Effective and deadly, she only had to use the throat strike once to defend herself in a fight to keep their territory intact. Rocco also had taught her how to fire guns to defend herself but whenever possible she left the dirty work to the brutes—not that her conscience was clear. She'd done her fair share of things that kept her up at night. For the simple fact of preserving her own life while she resided in the wolf's den, she'd resorted to taking sleeping pills at night to ward off the demons—not something she was happy about.

With his gun out, Sammy approached the door with the crew behind him. In one swift kick, the door flew open with ease, smashing into the opposite wall. The two male occupants inside rose from the couch with shock on their faces. The bigger one in front lifted his arm to reach for something behind his back. Sammy reacted by aiming his gun at him.

"No!" Luke pushed Sammy's outstretched arm away and leaped toward the big guy to subdue him.

Sammy grunted as he fell over from the momentum to the ground.

The smaller guy, Joe Manero, lunged at Sophia, arms out as if to grab for her. "So, the boss came out of hiding?"

"I came out of hiding to deal with you," she said, punching him in the jaw before he could get a grip. Adrenaline coursed through her body, dulling the pain in her knuckles.

Joe grabbed his face as he stumbled backward.

"We only come out to deal with the rats," Kid said, taking the opportunity to try and rush him to the ground.

"Then I'm a rat that's faster than you," Joe said with gritted teeth and fury in his eyes. Side-stepping past Kid, Joe pounced again at Sophia.

As she turned to run out the door, her foot caught the corner edge of the rug, slowing her body down enough for Joe to slam into her. A groan escaped her lips as she fell to the ground, smacking her head on the corner of the coffee table.

Pain shot through her body like lightning bolts exploding in her flesh. The room became blurry as she felt his weight on her. She struggled to move but the force on her muscles incapacitated her. Fingers encircled her throat, squeezing her windpipe. Panic made adrenaline pump through her veins as she scratched and pulled at the hands around her neck. But nothing helped. Her body went limp as the air supply dwindled to zero.

With the little consciousness she had left, she heard

shouts and what sounded like a struggle. The vise around her throat loosened. Air forced its way back into her body, awakening her mind. The immense mass left her torso and for a second she'd thought she'd gone to the other side until she recognized Luke's voice.

"Get off her!"

Sophia coughed and gasped for air as she watched him toss Joe around until he stopped fighting back.

"Is everyone all right?" Sammy asked with a black duffle bag over his shoulder.

"We are now. You got the money?" Kid asked as he tied up Joe's hands behind his back.

"Yeah, once I saw things were under control here, I went to look for it. They hid it in the ceiling panel like we would." Then he turned to their prisoners. "This is the last time we ever do any business with you two." He pointed at Joe and the larger man. "We should whack them and be done with it."

"There's no need," Luke said, kneeling down in front of Sophia. "You got your money. They're not going to say anything."

Sammy cocked his head. "That seems risky. They could retaliate or snitch. It's best to make them disappear."

"Enough bloodshed," Luke said. "They won't talk. If they do, you can come after me."

Sammy stared down at Luke. "You bet I will. I'm not sure I agree but I like your confidence, Fighter."

"I'm thrilled." Then he turned toward Sophia. "Do you need a hospital?"

Still in a seated position with her hands around her throat, Sophia struggled to find her voice. Instead, she shook her head.

"Are you sure?"

"Yes." Her voice came out raspy.

He grabbed her hands and helped her stand.

Even though she wasn't ready, she was grateful for him helping her to save face amongst her subordinates. "Thank you," she whispered. She knew she had a long road toward healing.

Sammy broke the uncomfortable silence. "Where were you?" He lashed out at Kid. "If Luke hadn't stepped in, our boss would've been in a world of trouble. Isn't that your job? To protect the boss?"

"What do you mean?" Kid said, with his arms out. "I went after Joe. Ask Sophia. I can't help it he's a slippery rat."

"You didn't do enough," Sammy said, shaking his head.

"All right, all right," Sophia croaked. "Let's go. We can talk about it later."

On the ride back to her house sitting in between Sammy and Luke again, Sophia's emotions twisted around in her mind. Although she'd seen her fair share of violence growing up, she'd never come this close to dying. Yet, instead of her trusted, experienced thugs coming to her rescue, it was the new recruit, Luke, who had saved her.

She fought the urge to reach out and intertwine her fingers within the safety of his for the rest of the night. Maybe for once she could close her eyes and feel as if her sleepless nights would end with him around to banish the demons—an impossible wish. She would lose respect among the crew, and her status as the boss would be seriously questioned. They might even have her killed for deviating so far from the norm. Having a woman for a boss was already pushing the limits but proving to everyone why it had been a bad idea in the first place was even worse. She leaned her head against the headrest, closing her eyes, wondering if she was willing to take the risk of losing everything and walk away for a chance at a different life and have a shot at being truly happy. She knew she would.

Chapter Seven

During his afternoon shift at the Prickly Cactus, Luke stared at a bag of potato chips he'd packaged up for a customer, he flashed back to the ride home from Joe Manero's house. He'd noticed Sophia's longing glances in his direction but wasn't sure what to make of it. As much as he wanted to give in to her advances, he was certain *he* wasn't her escape route—quite the opposite. The way she looked at him made him want to grab her and run away from all their problems—an impossible option.

"Sir?" the elderly customer with unkempt white eyebrows said, waking him out of his trance.

"Sorry." He quickly placed the last item, a bunch of green onions, on top of the potato chip bag and grabbed the shopping bag handles, wincing as he handed the bag to the man. The skin on his right knuckle stung every time he closed his hand. He'd been nursing his wounds for the past few days while Sophia recovered in her home. "Have a nice day."

The customer didn't smile as he took the bag and promptly exited the store.

"And are you having a nice day, Fighter?" Sammy announced, strolling into the grocery store.

Luke's heart stopped. "Sammy, you found me." If Sammy could so easily learn where he worked, how long until they discovered the recording device?

The cashier, Benny, took one look at Sammy and scurried away into the backroom for a break.

"You have quite an effect on people," Luke told him.

Sammy smiled. "That's what I'm told. You work here, Fighter?" he asked as he scanned the small sparse shop with his good eye.

"Part time. I can't make a living running errands for you."

"Fair enough. I thought, based on your proposal to us, that you'd be doing something a little more…lucrative."

Luke put his hands out. "That's what I'm hoping for. Maybe you could put in a good word for me with the big kahuna."

"All in good time. I shouldn't tell you this, but your performance so far has been pretty good."

"Glad to hear it."

He'd left the recording device back at his apartment, not expecting this meet-up with Sammy but even if he'd worn it at this point, he knew Sophia's crew trusted him enough not to search or suspect him. Even though his freedom was on the line, his stomach soured with the guilt he had from helping bring them down. Strangely enough, he seemed to be good at being in the mafia—an outcome he hadn't expected and didn't know how to process. And while wearing the wire was not negotiable, he didn't have to like it.

"I don't want to get you fired, so I won't keep you any longer," Sammy said. "I think your co-worker might be close to calling the cops."

Luke chuckled. "How did you find me, anyway?"

"It was easy. I had someone follow you."

"That's comforting."

"Don't worry about it, Fighter. We trust you."

Luke studied Sammy's expression, looking for any signs of suspicion. He saw none. "What time do you get off work?" Sammy asked.

"In about an hour."

"Come by Frank's Gym after work. We've got something lined up for you."

Luke sucked in an exhausted breath.

With a hint of mischief in his good eye, Sammy smiled wide. "I promise you're going to really enjoy this. It's right up your alley."

"Am I going to need a lot of recovery time after? I have a few more shifts this week."

Sammy bared his teeth. "Put it this way, I've got my money on you. All you need to do is win."

Luke shook his head. "All right."

Sammy turned to leave. At the door he stopped to face Luke once more. "Wear some workout clothes."

Luke frowned but didn't get an explanation from the man as he stepped out the door. Workout clothes. An unusual request given the crew were not exactly health fanatics.

Once Benny had come out of hiding in the back room and Luke was finally able to leave work, he made his way toward Frank's Gym after stopping off at his apartment to change into workout clothes as Sammy had instructed. Located in a strip mall just off the highway, he recognized the run-down facility as he had previously driven by it.

He turned down the road to park near the entrance of the gym, passing a seedy clothing store, a small deli, and a cheap fast-food joint. His skin prickled as he wondered why the crew had chosen this place. But then again, over the past several weeks he'd been called so many times to perform like a monkey, nothing should surprise him or seem off limits.

"Hey, Fighter!" Sammy announced as Luke reluctantly walked into the gym. "We've got a special surprise for you."

Luke marveled at the massive warehouse ceiling with mirrored walls. The stench of sweat burned his nostrils. The main area of the room had a well-used boxing ring with sagging ringside ropes and dark red droplets staining the center of the ring.

Sammy walked over with a pair of red boxing gloves tied together and slung over his shoulder. His good eye twinkled with mischief. "We know you can fight. Here's your chance to prove it."

Luke threw up his hands. "Man, this is crazy. I've never done any fighting in a ring before. I don't even know the rules."

"It's easy," Sammy said, handing over the gloves. "No hitting below the belt. No biting, headbutting, kicking, or spitting. There's nothing to it. Tony and some of the other crew are here, too. We've all got bets going in favor of you. We know you can win."

Luke's chin went up. "You've got money on this?"

"We're not worried at all. From what I've seen you can't lose."

"Who am I fighting?"

Sammy turned toward the men's locker room at the left corner of the gym. "Ivar! Come meet Luke."

Before Luke could protest further, Ivar slammed open the locker door and stalked with long strides toward them. He hadn't bothered to put a shirt over his lean, ripped abs, and his blond hair bounced into his face as he stomped his way across the floor.

Luke's chest tightened as panic set in. "An actual boxer? You have me fighting against a heavy weight?"

"Ivar may be a heavyweight champion but he's no match for you." Sammy slapped Luke in the back and then turned to face him, his one eye staring at him with intensity. "I'm not worried at all."

Luke tried not to flinch as Sammy squeezed his shoulders, while staring deep into his soul. "We've got a lot of money on this, Fighter. We need you to win this match—give it everything you've got. *Capisce?*"

Luke sighed. His body went numb. Although the matchup was clearly unfair, he had to win this for them, or they'd never make him a member of their crew. His heart slammed against his chest. No pressure, just conquer the tallest mountain ever climbed. "I've got this. Don't worry."

Sammy smiled and patted the back of Luke's neck. "Good. That's what I like to hear." Then he waved Ivar over. "Ivar, this is Luke. He's our champion and very important to us."

Ivar's steely blue eyes stared down at Luke, towering over him.

Luke recognized the tactic—intimidation. But from experience he knew that really meant lack of talent. Not needing to resort to tricks and games to win, he had the one thing that worked for him every time, heart.

"Let's go, fellas." Sammy walked over to the ring. "Ivar, you're in the red corner. Luke, you're blue."

Luke noticed Tony, Kid and a couple others from the crew sitting by the blue corner. A referee he didn't recognize stood at the center of the ring and an older man who resembled Ivar stood by the red corner. As Luke removed his sweatshirt, the guys encouraged him while patting him on the back. Kid stood off to the side, a bit removed and quiet. Luke shrugged it off as probably related to Sammy praising him over Kid after the collection incident. He'd deal with Kid later. At the moment he had bigger things to worry about in the form of a heavyweight champion boxer.

"You got this, Luke," Tony said, dressed in his usual gray suit.

Luke slowed his breathing and said nothing as he climbed into the ring. Ivar bounced around in his corner, staring at his opponent—seemed like a waste of energy.

The referee walked to the center and gestured to the two fighters to come toward him. "All right, fighters. Let's have a clean fight. You know the rules." He glanced back and forth between the two opponents. "Touch gloves and go back to your corners."

Ivar pushed his gloves hard into Luke's, almost making him stumble backward. The ref glared at Ivar as he moved to his corner. Then he motioned to the timekeeper to ring the bell.

As soon as the bell rang, Ivar charged like a bull toward Luke. His right hook met with air as Luke ducked out of the way and returned an uppercut to the chin. Cheers from his camp rang out. But Ivar's grunt meant he was pissed. He retaliated with a couple hard jabs to Luke's face. A trickle of blood ran down Luke's nose as he blocked the next set of punches. The metallic taste turned his stomach as he tried and failed to connect his strikes. Just before he thought he might go down, the bell rang. The onslaught ceased and he was able to retreat to his corner where Sammy had a large cotton swab ready to stick up his nose.

"You're doing great, Fighter. Don't let him intimidate you."

After spitting out some bloody saliva into a bucket, Luke drank deeply from a water bottle. "He's vicious."

"So are you. Don't you forget it. He likes to charge at his opponent. That's where you're going to get your hits in"—Sammy came around and looked him in the eye with fierce intensity—"over and over again until he falls down. You got it?"

Luke nodded.

Sammy took the cotton swab out of his nose and wiped the sweat from his brow. "Now get out there and fight!"

The bell rang and Luke shot up from his seat. As he forced the cobwebs from his mind, Sammy's determined face was all he could think about—and the money that was riding on him. As predicted, Ivar came stomping toward him. Luke breathed in a calm breath before the storm. He could do this. Ivar's muscular right arm seemed to be his weapon of choice but way too obvious. Luke ducked out of the way and clocked him with a right hook and then followed it with an unexpected left powerful jab to the eye that sent him stumbling backward to the floor. The referee started counting and motioned for Luke to go to his corner. He obeyed, bouncing around with adrenaline. This could be it.

"—Six, seven, eight—" the ref called out as Luke's corner hollered.

Ivar blinked a few times but couldn't raise his head from the ground.

"—Nine, ten. Knockout." The ref raised Luke's arm. "Winner."

As the crew lost their minds, Luke forgot all about Special Agent Troy Wilson, the recorder in his sock and the lies he'd been telling Sophia. In this moment he felt like he was part of the group, like he belonged to something special, something that had been missing in his life.

In this moment, he wasn't Luke Daniels, FBI informant and traitor. He was Fighter, talented boxer and respected member of the Costa Crew.

Chapter Eight

Sophia winced as she applied foundation to her bruised neck—serves her right, she grumbled, for thinking she could come out of hiding while a hitman yearned for her quick and lucrative death. Did she have any proof of a hit?

No, but why else would a routine collection turn so violent? Granted, it could have been the Esposito crew but somehow this felt different—more personal. She'd been the only one hurt and therefore she reasoned she must have been the intended target. And there was no one to blame but herself. She'd gotten caught up in Luke's initiation and threw caution to the wind—an irresponsible decision for a boss.

As she privately berated herself, she heard the doorbell ring. Not wanting to make the same mistake twice, her brain kicked into high gear. Jumping up from her vanity, she grabbed the loaded gun from the bottom drawer she kept for emergencies and raced down the stairs toward the front door. After the incident with the last money collection, Tony had checked on her more frequently—but this morning he'd gone out for some coffee and bagels. She'd have to deal with this on her own.

Holding the gun up, she squinted through the frosted glass panels adjacent to the front door, trying to detect any recognizable features of the person standing there. A tall lean man with light-colored hair stood calmly by the door. There weren't many in her immediate sphere who fit that description. She emptied her lungs of air but kept the gun at her side as she opened the door a small crack.

His sage green eyes scanned her face and then went straight to the gun. "After all we've been through?"

She grinned over the butterflies bouncing around her belly and let the door open, allowing Luke Daniels to walk into the foyer. "I never know who's trying to kill me these days."

"I can assure you today, it's not me."

Sophia studied the variations of purple near his eyes and the red marks over his bottom lip. "What happened to you? You look like you've taken a beating."

"You mean you didn't sanction the boxing match against the heavyweight champion, Ivar the Terrible?"

"No, Tony didn't tell me anything. I bet Sammy was the ringleader."

"He sure was, and he made sure to bet on me."

Sophia cocked her head. "Naturally. Did you win?"

"Of course."

She smiled. *Of course.* "Sammy knew what he was doing. I bet they're very pleased with you."

"I would think so. The odds were definitely against me."

"On the other hand, if you keep winning, this might become a regular thing. I'm not sure that's what you want."

"Bring it on. I can take it."

Unfazed by his unplanned appearance, she led him into the modern un-cluttered living room toward the beige couches surrounding a glass table.

"Nice place," he said, looking around the living

room.

She sat opposite him and placed the gun on the table between them. "It'll have to do until the weather improves—if you know what I mean."

His eyes fell on her neck. "How have you been holding up?"

"I'm healing." She glimpsed the horror on his face. "What can I expect hanging around those creeps all the time? I have to thank you for stepping in when you did. I probably wouldn't be here if you hadn't done something."

"I'm sure somebody would've done something to help you but I'm glad I was there. And I agree that it seems like a dangerous task to be involved with on a regular basis."

"That's the thing, this job *is* dangerous, but this felt different. That's why I've been thinking it was a setup. There has to be a connection between what happened at the collection and the hitman who's been after me."

Luke nodded. "Maybe. But how would they know about the collection? Unless there's someone on the inside who's feeding them that information?"

"It's possible." She shrugged. "I can name a few who don't like that I'm the boss, but I can't go around accusing people without proof. I might be the boss but I'm not stupid."

"Understood. When is the next collection?"

"In a week."

Luke's eyebrows shot up. "You can't go. The same thing will happen, if not worse. You should stay in hiding until the hitman is dealt with."

Sophia appreciated his concern. Lord knows all the tough guys in her life were never allowed to show any signs of weakness. Luke was different—a teddy bear under the bruises.

"I hear you, but I am the boss. How would that look? In fact, it might give them an excuse to get rid of me. Being the boss means that my position is constantly being questioned. All the members want that power and I'm sure some of them don't want a woman leading them."

"Your brother put you in a tough spot. I wonder if you can talk to him about the hitman threat. Surely, he must care that your life is in danger. Maybe he can give the position to someone else for your own safety?"

"I think about that every day." She shook her head. "But I know he won't do it. It's easier to justify giving the role to family. If he tried to give it to anyone else, they would fight over it. Keeping the peace in the organization always comes first."

"Even if your blood was on his hands?"

She nodded. "I can't explain it to an outsider. You can't back out just because there's some heat. We need to figure out who's putting out the hit and deal with them."

"How did you know about the hit placed on you in the first place?"

"About a month ago, I noticed suspicious behavior targeting me. I was getting the cold shoulder from certain crew members. Cars were following me everywhere I went but I couldn't figure out who was to blame and as soon as that started, Tony ordered me into hiding. He probably saved my life back then but it's just a matter of time before the opportunity to whack me presents itself, which is why we need to get to them first."

"I don't disagree, but it will be hard finding out

who's been disloyal."

"That's true. But who am I kidding? Tony's a great guy but I know they are all following my brother's orders. It's just a matter of time before one of them decides they've had enough." Sophia couldn't stop the tears from trickling down her cheek. She'd been holding onto so much fear and pressure, it was no surprise she was always on the cusp of breaking down. "I'm sorry."

Luke got up from his seat and sat down next to her. "Don't be sorry. None of this is your fault." He reached over and leaned in to embrace her.

She felt him rub her back gently. Her body relaxed as she breathed in the scent of aftershave. This was wrong. A new recruit hugging the boss alone in her home—they'd be shot on sight. Their bodies would be quartered and dropped into the nearest lake. Yet, she didn't budge. Tony had the keys to her house and could walk in at any moment and catch them with horror plastered on his face. But she couldn't move. When was the last time anyone showed her a little compassion—a piece of their heart? Knowing all too well they were being bad, she greedily soaked up his merciful empathy and let him lead the way for once.

As they pulled out of their embrace, she noticed him staring down at her lips. Sophia remained still as he leaned in and gave her a soft kiss. Her lips detected the hard ridges from the broken skin of his wounded bottom lip. But he didn't flinch or move. Her stomach leaped into her throat, igniting a new desire for him she didn't know existed. Feelings of wrong and right swirled in her mind but she did nothing to stop it.

Until she heard the familiar grinding sound of keys entering the front door lock. Leaping to her feet, she announced, "Tony's back." Fleeing from the couch like a guilty criminal, she went to greet her advisor. She was a dead woman. All the efforts to stay alive and lead an entire crew had been squandered by her adolescent need to kiss the new recruit. She wanted to smack her own head and yell, *Wake up, Sophia!*

"Tony, you're back," she said, taking the white paper bag from him. "I see you got your breakfast?"

"I had to go to two different places to get the bagels. I like them chewy with a nice crisp outer layer."

She laughed too loud, closing the door as he entered. "A good bagel is hard to find around here."

Luke had gotten up and had made his way toward the front.

"Is that you, Fighter?" Tony asked.

"Hey, Tony. I came by to see how Sophia was doing after the collection and to tell her about my win."

"Uh-huh." He eyed them both. "Well, you can trust that I'm in charge of her well-being and you're busy enough being a new recruit. Sophia, you should've seen him out there. Look at his face. He took a real beating but won against a heavyweight. It was incredible."

She looked at Luke as he sheepishly made his way to the door to leave. "I bet it was a sight."

"Just doing what I'm told," Luke said, raising his shoulders with his hands in his pockets.

"Ah," Tony said, waving his hand dismissively. "You're too modest."

"Maybe I can check out the next fight," she said, throwing caution to the wind, unable to control herself.

Luke paused in front of the door but refused to make eye contact. "Yeah...maybe next time," he mumbled to the ground and walked out.

Sophia looked at Tony, hoping he wouldn't say another word about what he may have witnessed between her and Luke.

"Let's go toast up those bagels," he said, taking the bag from her. "I'm starving."

She let out the breath she was holding and smiled in relief. "Me too. Great idea."

Chapter Nine

"I need more." Troy Wilson said as he bit into a strip of crispy bacon. "All I've got is evidence of rough housing. There's barely any conversation at all."

"We went on a collection run. There should've been something on that recording." Luke knew he had stopped Sammy from whacking the two guys and getting himself into real trouble. Why he had done that was the real question.

"There was a fight. I heard you were clearly playing the hero. We can bring charges based on the recordings, but we want something bigger. We need evidence that will clearly stick in court."

Luke knew when he walked into the diner in the morning that Troy wouldn't be happy with the recording. Not only did he not wear the wire during his boxing match with Ivar, but he'd also left it at home when he visited Sophia—no doubt that had been the right decision. He'd gotten himself in a deeper mess with her than he could ever imagine. If she ever found out he was a snitch, there were two possible scenarios: she would hate him for his betrayal forever or she would have him killed—probably both. He honestly didn't know which was worse.

"I'm working my way up the ranks. You know they reserve their most incriminating conversations for private interactions. They have to trust me enough to say something that implicates them."

"I thought you were going to run the drug trafficking business for them."

"I haven't gotten that far. You know how it works; it takes time. I'm working on it. The other day they had me fighting an actual champion boxer to prove myself. I won, of course, but that's my point." Luke smiled, making his split lip ache. "They're testing me to see how far I'll go and if I'm worthy enough."

Troy narrowed his eyes. "Is that why you look like a truck ran over your face?"

"Is it that bad?"

Troy leaned in. "Tell me something, *Fighter*, are you starting to get too comfortable? I might be reading you wrong, but it seems like you're proud to be doing their bidding."

Luke shrugged. "I'm just happy I won the fight. That's all. Can't I have one moment of joy? Or do I have to suffer through every minute of this?"

"A moment of joy? What did you think this was? A carnival?"

Luke rolled his eyes in response.

"It also sounded on the tapes like you saved a damsel in distress in the form of the boss. Care to comment on that?"

Luke's head started to pound. Recapping the scene where Sophia almost died in his arms made him angry enough. To hear Troy presume he was romantically involved with the boss really made his blood boil. "She was specifically being targeted. What would you have done? Let her die?"

"It would certainly shake things up a bit."

There were no words, only reaction. Luke shot out

of his seat and grabbed Troy by his collar. "You *would* like that, wouldn't you? What's the matter? You've got some sick and twisted past you need to take out on someone?"

A hard jab to the stomach made Luke freeze as he realized Troy had aimed his gun at his guts. Releasing the man's collar, Luke pushed down his anger to preserve his life.

Troy looked around the empty diner and put his gun back in its shoulder holster. "You're lucky no one saw. Sit back down."

Luke dragged his hands through his hair and reluctantly returned to his seat. *That was dumb.* Not only did he reveal his true feelings, but he almost got himself killed.

Troy cleared his throat. "Look, I'm not a sociopath but I'll be honest, I think you're getting too close to the criminals. To answer your question, yes, I've had a few scenarios like this not turn out as planned. People died as a result. I want to be sure that if someone has to die, that person won't be one of ours. It's not abnormal to relate to the people you've been hanging out with day and night, but I want to be sure you won't turn tables and decide that you'd rather be with them. I also don't think you're wearing the device for every encounter with them for reasons that are unclear to me. This will take forever if you don't wear it."

"I'll wear it. I'll wear it." He struggled to look Troy in the eyes, embarrassed by his behavior. "You really think I want to be part of the mafia?"

Troy raised his brow. "You're sure acting like you do."

Luke shook his head. "It's not true. I want my rap

sheet erased and move on with my life."

"And what does that life look like?"

Luke pushed down images of Sophia's lips. "I was always good with computers. Maybe I'll go back to school and start over—a new beginning."

Troy narrowed his eyes like he didn't believe a word. "If that's the case, then keep your eye on the prize, wear the recording device and get back to work."

****

The droopy skin under the eyes made Carmine Bruno's face resemble a bulldog. A massive cigar hung from the corner of his mouth, bobbing up and down as he spoke, sitting across from Sammy and Luke in the backroom of Lucky Guess.

"Vito D'Angelo is one of the new guys," Carmine explained. "He's an associate but well respected amongst the crew. You can't blame him for defending himself. I would do the same thing if someone smashed my door in and pointed a gun at me with no explanation."

"What was he doing with that piece of garbage, Joe Manero?" Luke spat. Visuals of Manero's skinny fingers around Sophia's neck flashed through his mind. He's lucky Luke had some self-control.

Sammy glared at Luke. "Manero will spend the rest of his life living in fear. That's worse than death if you ask me," Sammy said. "But I agree we weren't expecting a member of your crew to be hanging out with Manero, of all people."

"Vito's not a made man yet but that being said he wasn't doing anything wrong. In fact, he was acting in self-defense. As you know very well, when something like this happens, we need some retribution."

"Ah, come on, Carmine," Sammy said. "Normally,

you know we wouldn't be having this type of meeting. You might have your own crew, but you're still part of Sophia's group."

Carmine jabbed his index finger into the table. "I've been around since the days when Rocco Costa was first made boss. I've done my job and brought in tons of money. My crew is a separate entity from Sophia's that I recruited myself. As their boss, I owe them the same protection and respect you give to your guys."

"That's fine, Carmine, but my guys didn't know he was part of your crew. They were there to collect what they were owed," Sammy said, turning to Luke. "Manero went too far but Vito barely got hurt."

"It's true," Luke added. "Manero got the bulk of the attack. Vito was barely pushed. He probably doesn't even have a mark on him."

"They were tied up and left in the house for almost two days until Manero's sister found them," Carmine said. "If she hadn't stopped by, they'd both be dead."

Luke wanted to say good riddance but held his tongue while Sammy continued his diplomacy tour.

Sammy rubbed his eye patch—a nervous tic Luke noticed a while back. "What's it going to take?"

Carmine puffed on the cigar. The fumes burned Luke's nose, making him look away from their table. The backroom had been cleared out for their meeting, but he could still hear the jukebox in the front bar playing music from the eighties.

After a couple more drags, Carmine finally replaced the cigar on the edge of the ashtray as the plume of smoke rose to the ceiling. "I want an apology given to Vito personally."

Sammy glanced at Luke. "We can do that. We can

have Luke come along since he was heavily involved in the muscle power."

Carmine shook his head. "Nah, not from you two. The apology needs to come from your boss."

"Sophia?" Sammy straightened his back.

Luke bit his tongue. Every cell in his body wanted to fly over the table and slam into that ugly mug.

"Carmine, that's an unusual request," Sammy said. "We're prepared to offer Vito monetary compensation. That's a pretty good deal if you ask me."

"There's no negotiation. Sophia, as your boss, needs to personally deliver an apology to Vito at his residence. Or else."

"Or else what?" Luke spat.

Before he took another breath, Luke found himself staring at the barrel of the gun Carmine had whipped out of nowhere.

Sammy put up his hand. "Hold it! Now hold on. Calm down."

"Does this explain it for you?" Carmine shook the gun in Luke's face.

"I think we can arrange a meeting with Vito and Sophia if that's what it's going to take," Sammy said.

Carmine slowly pulled his gun away and replaced it inside his jacket.

Luke's heart pounded in his ears. He wasn't used to being on the receiving end of any gun, let alone one carried by the underboss.

"That's what it will take," Carmine said, getting up from his seat. "I'll be in touch with the details." He grabbed his cigar from the ashtray and popped it back in the corner of his mouth. "And she better show up alone."

Chapter Ten

Sophia's jaw dropped as she sat on her couch across from Sammy while he told her about the meeting they'd had with Carmine. Luke and Tony sat on opposite sides of her, knees bouncing in tandem.

"He wants an apology?" Sophia asked, noting Luke's somber mood.

Sammy nodded. "For attacking his guy Vito when we went to collect from Manero."

She stood, then walked over to the nearest window. The morning sun had cast shadows of long pointy sagebrush on the concrete road. She longed to be that still and calm.

"Sophia, none of us knew Vito was in Carmine's crew," Sammy explained. "If we had known, we wouldn't have touched a hair on his head. The guy's not even a real member. I say we go over to Vito's today, get this over with and move on."

Annoyed that her own crew had basically thrown her under the bus, she ignored him and walked over to the kitchen. She busied herself with removing a charcuterie board filled with meats and cheeses from the fridge. Bringing the platter over to the table, she placed it in front of her men and sat down. "Can I get anyone a drink?"

Tony popped a few pieces of cut-up parmesan into his mouth. "You got the good kind, too."

Luke chuckled.

"Why would I get anything else?" she asked. "Have you tried the salami? Aged to perfection."

"No, salami has too much fat in it. I'm watching my figure," Tony replied. "What about you, Fighter, you like salami?"

Luke shook his head. "Not really. It gets stuck in my teeth."

"Are you kids done with snack time?" Sammy asked.

"It's better than talking about my impending death," Sophia said. "This is exactly what Carmine wants me to do—show up at their doorstep unprotected, ready to take the shot he's been planning all along."

The men were silent as Sammy blinked his good eye. "What's he planning?"

Sophia stood up and began pacing. "You know as well as I do, Carmine wanted Rocco to make him boss but when he made me boss instead, he got pissed."

"Yeah, but he's got his own crew now," Sammy replied.

Sophia closed her eyes in response. "You're always sticking up for him, Sammy. It makes me think you've got something going on the side with him."

Sammy's one eye went wide. "I've got no stake in this fight. I'm trying to keep the peace and if you think—"

"All right, all right," Tony interjected. "Let's not get crazy here. Sophia, are you saying you think Carmine's out to whack you?"

Her arms spread wide. "Who isn't trying to whack me? And he's got more of a motive than all the others because he wants to be boss."

Tony snickered but Sophia could see from Luke's pout that he wasn't thrilled by her comment.

"I don't agree, but fine," Sammy said and shrugged. "Let's say he is trying to squeeze you out in the hopes Rocco will make him boss, we still need that apology to move on."

"We should whack him," Luke said.

Both Tony and Sammy looked at him.

"Everyone calm down," Tony said. "There's an order to things. We can't just go whacking everyone and everything. The Feds would love that. If we can give this apology without anyone getting hurt, that would be the best scenario."

"Carmine wants her to go alone," Sammy said.

"That's not possible," Tony said. "We can make it look like she's gone to Vito's house alone, but she'll have backup waiting in the wings in case Carmine has other plans. That's the only way this makes any sense."

"If Carmine finds out she wasn't alone," Sammy warned, "he could start an all-out war in retaliation."

Tony held up his hand. "This is non-negotiable. Sophia's not going alone. If she does, it will be over my dead body."

"It might come to that," Sammy said.

Tony shrugged. "Fine. I'll take the hit but in no way is her murder going to be on my watch. Now, who's going with her?"

"I am," Luke said without hesitation.

****

The recording device stayed hidden in Luke's apartment under the loose floorboard he'd discovered while he paced the floor shortly after meeting up with the Costas. Even though Troy would be pissed at the lack of intel, he didn't want to record a murder by his own hands—if it came to that.

The silence in the car as he drove Sophia over to Vito's house spoke volumes. His stomach churned with unease, but he wouldn't let her see he was genuinely worried about her safety.

"It's rather foolish of Carmine," Sophia said, breaking the silence. "Did he really think I was going to show up by myself? Would a boss make that kind of decision?"

"That's what he demanded, and he probably assumed you would believe this would be a harmless meeting to settle affairs between members." He shrugged. "And maybe it will be or maybe not."

He could feel her eyes on him as he watched the road. Troy had loaned him the small white car while he worked undercover. He'd complained that the car seemed a bit feminine for him, but Troy insisted the car was standard issue. Luke was sure he'd done it to tease him.

"You seem down today," she asked. "Is something wrong?"

He'd spent most of the night tossing and turning as he agonized over the decision to stop pursuing her. The guilt from all the lies he'd told her to get himself out of doing any jail time tortured him all night until he'd finally convinced himself he needed to back off. And now, with his head pounding from lack of sleep, driving her to a death trap didn't brighten his mood.

He let out the breath he'd been holding. "I think we should cool it for a little while…in front of the guys." As soon as he said it his stomach dropped. It's not what he wanted. "I don't think we should add another layer to our

73

issues."

"I didn't realize you thought *we* were an issue," she bit back.

"It's complicated—"

"Oh, it's not you, it's me? Right?" She looked him dead in the eyes with a laser focus. "Why did you kiss me?"

He broke her gaze to watch the road and hide his embarrassment. "I kissed you because I couldn't resist. I meant everything I've said to you but it's not the best move for either of us." In this case it really was him, not her, getting in the way of their relationship as clichéd as it sounded. "The only thing I've ever wanted for you is to be safe and happy."

She let out a tiny snicker. "Don't worry about me. I've survived in the mafia all my life and not one bullet scar to show for it."

"That might change today."

"I don't believe that."

"Why?"

"I've got you on my side."

Could his head hurt any worse?

That was the problem; he wasn't on her side even if he desperately wanted to be. There was nothing left for him to say. He couldn't tell her the real reason why their relationship was based on lies—she'd probably have his head blown off before the Feds could even do anything about it. And it hurt.

Troy was right. He'd developed feelings for someone completely unavailable to him—not one of his smartest moves.

But as they approached Vito's house, he pushed his feelings deep inside and entered combat mode, knowing that this could be the end for both of them. The idea that they would go down together did give him some comfort.

Luke inched the car down the block. Vito's house was the last one on the left. It was a small brick house with unkempt bushes surrounding it and a set of concrete stairs leading up to the white door. There was nothing defining about the house and its size and appearance made it seem as if the man lived alone. A small green car was parked in the driveway, likely Vito's car.

"Doesn't seem like an ambush," Luke said.

"That's exactly how they want it to look," she said. "It reminds me of the time Sammy's brother, Marco, got killed while he waited in the car for Sammy to come out of a collection a few years ago. Car bomb. That's why Sammy would prefer to keep the peace. Losing his brother annihilated him. He never talks about it."

Luke stared at her. "That's awful. You'd think he'd want to be more cautious given what happened."

"I think he's in denial and being more cautious would probably feel like he's caving into his fears."

"That's totally irrational."

Sophia shrugged. "Maybe. This is what we signed up for and I know in my heart Carmine wants me taken out."

"But if that were true, how would that work? If Rocco learned Carmine was involved, he'd retaliate on his crew."

"Carmine would probably blame Vito for the ambush and use him as the sacrificial lamb. It'd be hard to prove anything on the contrary."

"Don't you get tired of these games?"

She nodded. "Very much. I can only hope someday things will be different for me."

He stared into the mysterious blue depths of her eyes. Her confidence against all odds astounded him. And, boy, was she stubborn.

"Now, do we have a plan or are we going to sit in the car all day?" she asked, breaking the awkward silence.

"It's not a very good one. I can't go with you because Vito won't open the door if he sees me. But I plan to move the car closer once you're inside and then I'll come up to the door after he closes it so I can break in if I need to."

She cocked her head. "Not great, but not the worst plan I've heard."

He let her comment slide, knowing she was used to being in charge. "Thanks." Searching her face, he wondered if she was masking fear. "You're not scared?"

"No," she said but avoided making eye contact.

He could tell she was lying. "I'll be one second away regardless."

She opened the passenger door. "I know you will." Then she headed toward the house.

Luke opened the glove compartment and reached for the gun Tony had loaned him. He should probably get his own, but he hadn't planned on continuing his life of crime for very long. Confirming the gun was loaded as Tony had told him, he weighed his limited options. Up until now, for his own conscience, he'd made it a point not to kill anyone during his time as an informant, but in this case, he wouldn't hesitate for a second.

As he watched Sophia climb the stairs, his eyes caught some movement reflecting off his left side mirror. A large black sedan was speeding down the street toward the house. The hairs on his neck stood up. It was an ambush. They were going to gun her down as she walked toward the front door.

"Sophia! Get down! It's an ambush!" he screamed out the window, throwing his gun down on the passenger seat while pushing on the accelerator. He swung the steering wheel to the left, effectively using his car as a barricade to stop the sedan from getting any closer to the house. Grabbing the gun, he lowered his window and fired off a few rounds directly at the car, hoping to stop them.

A few of the shots managed to crack the windshield but the dark car kept coming at him at high speed without any sign of slowing. Once he heard the click of an empty chamber, he lowered his gun realizing he did not have enough time to jump out of the car to safety. He wasn't a particularly religious man but with one second until impact, Luke closed his eyes and said a quick prayer as everything went black.

Chapter Eleven

"The prick still looks handsome even with his face smashed in," Sammy said, staring down at Luke in his hospital bed.

He tried smiling in response to Sammy's joke but winced instead, reminding him he'd been hit dead-on with a vehicle. His injuries had been bad enough to earn him a private room, which he was grateful for ever since the screaming coming from the waiting room began early in the morning.

Sophia's face appeared in his peripheral vision. Her mascara had run down her cheeks and her signature red lipstick had all but disappeared. "The doctors said you were very lucky. In fact, they said the black sedan had slowed down once they realized you weren't going to move out of the way."

"Remind me never to play poker with you," Sammy said.

"You're on," Luke croaked.

Tony laughed from the end of the bed. "Listen, Fighter, we slipped the nurse a little cash to get you this room and a bit of extra attention."

Luke's eyebrows shot up. "Wow, you shouldn't have. There are some perks after all."

"You bet," Sammy said. "Especially after a performance like that. We want to make sure you know we appreciate you."

A wave of delirium overcame him as the pain medication kicked in. He struggled to focus through the brain fog, but he could barely contain the enormous amount of affection he felt for his comrades. "I'm truly honored."

"The ambush proves what I've been saying all along," Sophia pressed. "Carmine wants me out."

"I believe you now, but he'll get away with it," Sammy said. "We have no idea who was in the black car since they sped off after the crash and no one else was seen on the premises. By now that car is in a landfill somewhere, crushed to the size of a tin can. Vito never opened the door to his house, and Carmine had an alibi."

"Forget the police," Sophia spat. "*We* know who's involved and *we* should do something about it before they try again."

"That might cause an all-out war," Sammy said.

"So be it," Sophia said.

"All our businesses will be in jeopardy. The whole organization will implode. Is that what you want?" Sammy asked her.

"Maybe. Maybe it's time we all get out and go our separate ways before the Feds catch up with us."

Luke watched as everyone fell silent. When he emerged from unconsciousness not too long ago, he could barely see through his swollen eyes. He did notice that his left arm was in a cast. The pain was like nothing else he'd experienced and in his fragile state, he agreed with Sophia. He wanted out of this situation badly. Even while being aware the minute his opportunity to be an informant went away, the closer he was to jail time. "I think this type of beef will never go away as long as Sophia is the boss. Maybe she should step down and let

Carmine take the position," he managed to croak.

"Oh boy, this guy really hit his head hard," Sammy said. "Maybe we should call the nurse over. He's really lost his mind."

"Yeah, Luke, what are you saying?" Tony asked. "Carmine was passed over for a reason. We don't want him in charge."

Luke tried rolling his eyes, but the swelling prevented him. Of course they don't want Sophia to step down. She lets them run the place. Carmine would rule with an iron fist.

"Besides, I think this episode will scare Carmine off for a bit. Thanks to our Fighter over here." Sammy said, playfully knocking on Luke's cast.

He winced in response. "For a short time, maybe."

"I think we should all let the dust settle," Sammy said. "Vito didn't get his apology, but Sophia was almost mowed down, and Luke is in the hospital. If you ask me, it's a wash. And I bet Carmine will agree."

"Fine," Tony said. "Let's hope so and let Fighter get some rest. I don't know about you guys, but hospitals give me the creeps."

"Really? Why?" Sammy asked.

"It's all the beeping noises and smells."

"Smells?"

"Yeah, you get two options in hospitals." Tony put two fingers up. "Cleaning solutions that burn your throat or smells so putrid, you'll never get it out of your mind."

"That's a bit dramatic, Tony," Sophia said.

"I don't know how you can smell anything over that cheap cologne you wear," Sammy said.

Luke laughed but immediately stopped himself when the pain sliced through him like a knife.

"Enough about Carmine and my cologne," Tony said. "Let's let Fighter get some rest. Sophia, I'll be waiting right outside."

"Thanks, Tony," she said as she watched everyone clear the room.

Luke heard her deep sighs as she used a tissue to wipe the mascara from her cheeks. She sniffed as the door to the room shut behind Tony. Then she stared down at Luke, studying his various injuries. "What a mess."

"Is it that bad?"

"I know you want to pump the breaks between us, and I understand why but how can I repay you?"

Her glassy jeweled eyes were still the most beautiful shade of blue he'd ever seen—or maybe it was the pain medication. "You can repay me by walking away and rebuilding your life. Do me a favor and go off to New York to work at that fashion company. I might get fewer injuries in the future."

She laughed. Then her mood darkened. "I wouldn't even know how to begin. This is all I know."

"You know murder and pain. Why would anyone stick around?"

She nodded. "Call me a sadist."

He worried she didn't want to move on because of him. At this moment he couldn't fight that battle as well. "I'll call you a casualty."

"I guess that's better than a snitch or dropout."

His stomach tightened. He hated when her lifelong grooming came out like an untamed wild animal. It wasn't her fault. It was all she knew. In one instance she might kiss him with all the tenderness in the world but a second later pull out a gun and shoot his brains out without hesitation. Chills racked his body.

"At least a snitch has control over what happens to them."

She leaned in closer, eyes hard and fixed on him. "Not if I get my hands on them."

He breathed in, disappointed by her harshness. She'd been taught cruelty was the answer to her problems. "And then what? You'll be just like them. Is that what you want?"

Her eyes softened but then filled with tears once again.

"What's wrong? What did I say?"

She sniffed, her gaze dropping to the floor. "You don't get it." She shook her head.

"Get what? I didn't mean to upset you. I know you are better than them."

Then she looked at him resolute and unyielding like a soldier sworn to uphold their allegiance. "You don't get it. . .I am them."

****

Over the past several days, Sophia had thought long and hard about Luke's recruitment into the group. He was an outsider, but he'd done more for the crew than anyone had in recent years. Admittedly, she was biased. And she knew how it looked to the others. The boss had the hots for the new recruit, and she needed her brother's blessing to make that recruit a member of the crew. That was why she hopped on a short flight to Colorado, rented a car, then drove to meet with her brother, Rocco, for his opinion. She figured if he approved of his recruitment into the group, the rest of the crew would rally behind the idea—and she might get what she wanted.

It wasn't the first time she'd visited Rocco in prison

but no matter how many times she'd seen it, the massive structure left her in awe. Isolated in between the surrounding majestic mountains, she imagined the prisoners must feel detached from the world, not unlike the way she felt at times—shackled to her role at the top.

She parked the car in the parking lot and entered the facility, her skin prickly with nervous energy. After the formalities of checking in, which included a search of her purse, she was led to a room with row after row of seating areas with plexiglass separating the inmate from the visitor. She sat in a chair and waited for Rocco to be brought into the room. Her black blazer hugged her waist, holding her back straight. This was a business meeting after all. She flung her slouchy purse around the back of her chair and watched as the correction officers brought Rocco into the meeting area. The handcuffs and leg chains clinked as he shuffled toward her. Sweat formed above her top lip. The enormous pressure to please her older brother resurfaced as if they were kids again and he bossed her around.

He cracked a smile as he sat down and grabbed the phone receiver off the console while she did the same on her side of the plexiglass. "Sophia, how've you been?"

"Not bad. Not great. You're looking well though."

He nodded. "I do what I can. There's no beauty salon in here, you know?"

She smiled.

"I heard some things," he continued. "It's rough out there."

"Not as rough as it is in here, I bet."

He shrugged, slumped in his chair. "Nothing I can't handle. How's Ma?"

"She acts tough, but I know she cries a lot. She's

worried she's going to be left all alone. You'll be in here and something bad will happen to me."

"You tell her I'll never leave her. On my word." Pulling his chest back in a very familiar gesture, he jabbed his pointer finger on the table. "There's a reason you're in this situation."

She was acutely aware their conversation was being recorded and Rocco was being as vague as possible; she understood him completely.

"Sophia, I know you're smart. You'll do the right thing and not get yourself into trouble."

"I'm not sure about that but I did want to come out here and make sure you were in agreement with everything that's gone on recently."

He stared at her without blinking. "I trust your instincts. After all, they should be similar to mine." Then he smirked, another familiar gesture.

She let out her breath, staring at her feet. "Sometimes I wonder if we do think the same way."

As soon as the words left her mouth, she wished she could take it back. The last thing she needed was for Rocco to think she wasn't one hundred percent behind the crew and its cause. If he wanted, he could have her ousted from the group as a traitor—or worse, sanction her death.

"Nah, I know you like the back of my hand. You need to show more confidence in yourself. I have no issues at all with how you are handling things. Although—"

Her heart stopped.

He leaned toward the plexiglass. "You look like you've lost some weight. I've been trying to find you a man worthy enough, but you've got to keep up your strength."

Smiling at his attempt at light conversation, she swallowed the lump in her throat. If he had any knowledge of what had been going on between her and Luke, this meeting would have a very different tone. "The good ones are hard to find."

"You can't be so picky. Time's ticking and you still have your looks. It'll be good for you to settle down and then we can reconsider the roles in the household."

Her stomach roiled. She wasn't entirely sure, but it sounded like Rocco was suggesting the role of boss could be transferred to her future husband. She knew that plan wouldn't make things better—in fact, probably worse. On one hand, going from mob boss to mob wife relieved the enormous pressure she'd had to deal with. But ceding independence and authority to another didn't seem appealing.

"If I approve, of course," he added. "That's why it can't be anyone off the street. He's got to be great."

Her mind whirled as she prayed he had no one for her. "And do you have someone in mind?"

"I might. I've been meaning to set up a meeting for you to get to know each other."

She folded her hands in her lap, squeezing them so tight her knuckles hurt. "Rocco, now's not the time. There's so much going on. I can't even come and go as I please."

"As you please?" His eyebrows shot up. "Everyone has to sacrifice a little to keep the household in order. Look at me. You think this is easy?" he asked as he tried and failed to yank his handcuffed hands apart. "I understand you've been having a hard time but it's not about the individual. There's a whole picture that I need to constantly think about to survive. *Capisce?*"

There was no arguing with him, but all this meeting did was solidify what she already knew—Rocco may be carrying around chains, but she remained shackled to the organization—truly unbearable. And she needed a way out.

"How's Vittoria?"

"Not happy. I don't blame her. Ever since you've been in here, she doesn't know what to do with herself."

He waved his hand. "Oh, I don't believe that. When I was on the outside, my wife was doing nothing but shopping and hanging out with her girlfriends. What's changed?"

"I think she feels like everyone pities her since you were incarcerated. She has to do everything with the kids and the house by herself."

"It's better than being here. You don't think I would give anything to be dealing with the kids and the house? Maybe that's how *you* think but that's not my wife."

She cocked her head. "Rocco?"

"What? You're the one who doesn't want to settle down. Maybe you're the one who doesn't want to deal with a house and kids."

"All right. That's enough. Vittoria's fine. I'm sure she misses you."

"Tell her I miss her too and she should come visit me more often."

She nodded.

"It's nice to see you, Sophia. I'm glad you stopped by. You're doing a good job from what I've heard."

As long as Tony didn't rat on her to Rocco, she'd live another day. "Thank you, Rocco. I'm doing my best."

He got up as the guards came to bring him back to his cell. "I'll have my guy set up a date with you. It's time to move on with your life."

"I can't wait." She stood up, her legs barely holding her up.

"Oh, and Sophia?" He turned his head around as the two guards came around on each side to lead him back inside. "Tell Luke I'll take him on in a boxing match any day." Without a smile or wink, he turned his back to her and let the guards take him back to his cell.

Sophia's blood went cold, her mouth dry as ash. "You won't win," she said to herself.

Chapter Twelve

Shoving the recording device into his sock, Luke reversed his rental car out of the parking lot in the back of the Prickly Cactus and made his way to Frank's Gym. Troy had promised him a new manly loaner car since the small white one had been totaled in the ambush. It'd taken a couple of weeks, but he was mostly recovered from the effects of the head-on collision with Carmine's crew. The guys had mostly left him alone during that time.

Until now.

Before he'd left his job at the store, he told the owner he needed to leave a bit early.

"Listen, Luke, you're scaring the customers," Larry told him while rubbing his frizzy beard.

"What do you mean?"

The owner squinted, cocked his head to one side. "What happened to your face?"

"Oh, it's a lot better than it was. My eyes were practically swollen shut. Broke my arm in two places and was picking glass out of my skin for days."

Larry scrunched up his tan, wrinkled face. "What happened? Are you getting into fights? I should tell you we don't tolerate that here."

"No, it was a car accident. I got sideswiped." Luke shook his head. "Craziest thing."

"Uh-huh." Larry stared at him with cloudy pale blue

eyes. "That's some sideswipe."

"Yeah, but I'm looking at a full recovery, so that's good."

"Glad to hear it. What happened to the other guy?"

Luke shrugged. "I don't know. It was a hit and run."

"They didn't catch the guy?"

"Nope."

"All right, well, I bring it up because Benny's a little nervous around you and your friends. It would be best if you didn't bring them around here."

"Oh sure, no problem."

Luke didn't want to argue with Larry. He needed the work, but he didn't quite understand how Troy managed to get him the job without Larry knowing what might come through the door. He couldn't be the first informant referred to the Prickly Cactus by Troy. Luke didn't want to ask too many questions and it seemed he and Larry would mutually play the game of ignorance. But eventually someone was bound to get shot.

Once he'd left Prickly Cactus, his mind turned to his next mission. Even though he enjoyed boxing and missed it for the most part, he hoped he hadn't been summoned for another round with yet another heavyweight boxer—his face and other wounds hadn't quite fully healed yet. But as he entered the dimly lit gym complex, with the crew standing around staring at him, blood rushed through his veins in a flight or fight response. The mood inside seeming more like an inquisition than a competition.

"Fighter, glad you could make it," Sammy said, beckoning him over to the ring where the rest of the crew had gathered.

Luke noticed they hadn't bothered to turn on all the

lights in the gym, ominously sinking some of the crew into the shadows.

"What's this all about?" he asked, acutely aware of how grossly outnumbered he was and that he may not make it out alive. At least the recording device might signal the Feds to come help him. Or maybe not.

"We're glad you're feeling better and your contributions to the crew have not gone unnoticed, but the fellas had some concerns," Sammy continued, while the others remained quiet and somber.

Head pounding, Luke unconsciously cradled his recovering left elbow. "What kind of concerns?"

His mind turned to the snitch conversation he'd had with Sophia in the hospital. Had she figured it out and blown his cover after he had basically dumped her? His eyes scanned the gym for the exits. He could make a break for it and would likely get pretty far ahead of this out-of-shape boozy group but then what? Eventually they would find him and scatter his remains over the desert—not how he wanted to go.

"Some of the guys think you've been pulling our legs."

Luke kept waiting for Sammy to break out in laughter and then bring out the drinks and party girls, but he quickly realized he'd probably be waiting forever. He crossed his arms defiantly over his chest. "How so?"

Before Sammy could say anything, Kid stepped forward from the others. "It doesn't add up. You came out of nowhere wanting to be part of this group. You fight like you've been professionally trained. Truth is, Luke Daniels, we think you're working for the government."

Luke's knees almost buckled. Every fiber of his

being struggled to hold his body up. "How could you think that? After I've busted my butt for weeks for you." His voice rose and for once he didn't care. "Fighter, get me a beer. Fighter, wash my car," he mimicked. "Get me some dinner—at one in the fricking morning, I might add." He spread his aching arms. "Damn it! All for what?"

Silence dominated the room.

"We want some more proof," Kid persisted.

"How can I give you that? I thought the Costa Crew was all about the value of your word and trust in the family."

"It is, but we haven't officially made you part of the family," Sammy said.

Luke walked over to the nearest heavy bag and gave it a punch with his good arm hard enough to send it swinging. " I've done everything you've asked. This is the thanks I get?"

"Now, now," Sammy said. "We like what we've seen so far but we need to be sure."

"Yeah, like I said, we need proof," Kid repeated, grinning from ear to ear.

Luke began to pace the floor, palms dripping with sweat while he waited for the latest instructions. Maybe if he told them he was blackmailed into wearing a wire they'd understand. Or, given that he'd earned enough respect, they'd reconsider the accusation.

Or, spend his last few minutes on this earth inside a stinking, dilapidated gym.

Kid looked him dead in the eye. "Strip."

"What?" Luke squawked.

"You heard me. Take your clothes off. We need to be sure you're telling the truth."

Luke chuckled. "You can't be serious. Come on, how about I'll fight anyone you want, and we'll forget the whole thing?"

Kid cocked his head. "We'll take your offer," he smirked, revealing his crooked teeth, "but you still have to strip."

Luke breathed in and sighed. "Fine. Let's get this over with." He peeled off his shirt, turned around a couple of times and threw it on the ground. "Happy?"

"That's good, Fighter but we've dealt with enough snitches to know those recording devices are small these days. They can be shoved anywhere."

Luke glared at Sammy. "Where exactly do you think I'd be willing to stick something like that?"

Sammy shrugged. "I don't know what you're willing to do but we can't be too careful."

Luke rolled his eyes. Maybe after his total humiliation they'll be embarrassed enough to leave him alone and not ask him to remove his shoes.

"Come on, Fighter. We don't have all day," Kid said.

"What if I refuse?" Luke asked.

Kid pulled a gun out from the inside of his jacket and pointed it at Luke. "If you refuse, I'll have to poke some holes in you."

Shaking his head, Luke raised both hands in a hold-on gesture. "This is totally unnecessary."

Kid shook the gun in Luke's face. "Do it."

"Fine. Enjoy the view." Luke bent over, yanked down both his pants and briefs in one shot and stood up, unable to look anyone in the eye.

While he stared at the ground, a beam of light shined directly on him as the gym's entrance door opened. Luke turned around toward the intrusion as the door promptly closed behind them. The unmistakable clicking sound of stiletto heels on the concrete floor announced who had interrupted them.

Luke didn't budge even though Sophia's eyes were fixed on him. Humiliation didn't quite cover what he was feeling. In fact, he hoped he would pass out to shut this scene down. But he could probably bet she was working even harder to contain her own embarrassment.

"Am I interrupting something?"

"We were testing his loyalty and making sure we didn't have a snitch on our hands," Sammy explained. "You can put your clothes back on now, Fighter. You're in the presence of a lady."

"I see," Sophia said, averting her eyes while he got dressed. "Did he pass the test?"

Sammy nodded. "He did all right."

"Well, good. Are we ready to make the announcement?"

"I think so," Sammy said.

Feeling less like an object to be toyed with, Luke noticed Kid cursing under his breath. What now? "I'm not making out with any of you, no matter how much you beg."

The crew collectively chuckled.

Sophia looked at him, her demeanor seemingly official. "This wasn't exactly how I planned to make this announcement, but I can't say I'm surprised with this group." She put out a hand. "Luke Daniels, we want to make you officially part of the crew."

Then she joined the rest of the crew as they whooped and cheered.

Luke couldn't believe his ears. He'd gone from

accepting his demise to reaching the ultimate goal in a matter of seconds. "Wow! I can't believe it. You guys really had me going there for a minute."

"Yeah, if we really thought you were a snitch, your head would be rolling on this dusty floor," Kid said.

"I bet."

"That's enough, Kid," Sophia scolded. "Let's wrap this up. The ceremony will be tomorrow. I expect all of you to be there." She stepped closer to Luke. "You thought you could get rid of me, but I won't let go so easily."

He cracked a slight smile, which quickly vanished. Becoming a member was key to getting the information the Feds wanted faster, but she was right, it would bring them closer. And that wasn't a good idea. "I see that."

She looked him up and down. "Nice briefs." And then she turned around, heels clicking as she walked out of the gym.

Chapter Thirteen

Sophia hesitated to light the last of several candles she'd placed around her basement bar. Though she felt conflicted about officially inducting someone she cared about into a life of crime, Luke's initiation ceremony into the Costa Crew should be a time for celebration. Once in, there was no way out.

On the other hand, this would bring him even closer to her, which she selfishly relished—especially after he told her to back off. Tears threatened to flood her cheeks whenever she replayed the scene in her mind of him telling her they should cool it in front of the guys. His fears and trepidations about their relationship were not unreasonable but since she had imagined a way out of this life with him there was no way she could let him go.

The alternative for her, as Rocco had outlined, was an arranged marriage to someone she wasn't attracted to—and a life she didn't want. And how had she planned on changing her future? She hoped Luke would win everyone over, including Rocco, and everything would fall into place.

"Penny for your thoughts?" Tony asked as he quietly made his way down the stairs dressed in one of his impeccable gray suits.

In the past she told him everything—but not this. "I might get clipped if I tell you."

He sat next to her at the black marble table in the

middle of the room. She'd placed the initiation materials at the center of the table and dimmed the lighting to set the tone.

He rubbed his chin as he seemed to be in contemplation. "There's still time to back out of this and still save face. You could say there's been a change of plan and cut him loose. No need to explain the reasoning to anyone."

Relieved to have someone on her side, Sophia smiled at Tony. He reminded her of her dad—gentle but smart—and dead at the hands of a rival crew member. It wasn't lost on her how she also faced the same fate as similar threats came at her from all sides.

"I can't. You have no idea how much I want to be reasonable but I'm afraid that's not in the cards for me."

"Listen, I know you didn't ask for this, but I told your dad that I would look after you and I think I've done my best. I won't be able to protect you from this." There was no sign of the playful twinkle in his eyes.

"I understand. You've done a great job. I don't know where I'd be without you and I'm willing to take the heat."

Tony shook his head. "Like father, like daughter."

A base board creaked as someone came down the stairs.

"Your security let me in," Luke said, looking like a million bucks in a brand-new black suit. His hair was still wet from a recent shower.

"You clean up pretty nice," Sophia said, letting discretion slip.

"It's the least I could do for this amazing honor."

Tony slapped Luke's back. "You deserve it, Fighter."

Luke nervously looked around the room. "What happens now? This looks serious."

"Have a seat at the table. I'll get *you* a drink this time." Tony made his way behind the bar. "Something stiff." He poured out a brown liquor into a tumbler and brought it over.

"Do I need to be coordinated for this?" Luke asked.

"Nah but try not to bleed all over the rug. It was imported."

"Bleed? Do I have to fight someone else?"

Sophia moved the wooden box on the table closer to her. "You're not fighting today." She opened the box and removed a small dagger with an ornate gold handle.

Luke eyed her with suspicion. "First the gun, now a knife? Tell me how you really feel?"

She didn't bat an eye. "This dagger has been used in every initiation ceremony performed for members of the Costa Crew. It's quite sacred."

Luke tossed the scotch down his throat and swallowed hard. "I'm ready when you are."

Impressed by his courage, she returned the dagger to the box. "Tony, where are the others?"

Tony looked at his watch. "Sammy should be here any minute. I can't promise Kid will come."

Sophia's nostrils flared. "Why not? He can't make that decision."

A galloping sound barreled down the basement steps. "Sorry I'm late," Sammy said slightly out of breath as he adjusted his tie. "I had to remind one of my clients what happens when they don't pay."

"You took care of it?" Tony asked.

Sammy stared at Tony with his good eye. "I got the money."

"Where's Kid?" Sophia asked.

"He said he's tied up and will try to make it when he can," Sammy answered.

"It's disrespectful." Tony shrugged. "We all know he's trying to make a statement by not showing up."

"We'll deal with him later. Let's begin." Sophia said, standing up with the dagger in her hand. She noticed Luke's eyes following her every move. It seemed he was willing to go wherever she led him. "Tony, do you have the words?"

Tony reached into his jacket pocket, pulled out a small document, and placed it in front of Luke.

"This is the oath you will take to become part of the Costa Crew." Sophia stared at him with intensity, shutting off her feelings to be the boss. "These words symbolize your commitment to us and your understanding of supreme loyalty to us until your death."

Luke looked down at the list in front of him.

Sophia began reciting the words as the others followed along.

Luke joined in and said, "I will be loyal to the members of the organization. I will always be available and on time for the organization. I will always pay what I owe and never steal from the organization. I will never cooperate with the authorities."

"You hear that, Fighter?" Sammy asked. "If you do get caught by the cops, you never tell them anything, even if you have to do time. You do your time like a man. *Capisce?*"

Luke nodded. "Of course."

After the oath, Sophia took the document and held it over a candle flame. It caught fire quickly, incinerating the secret words from existence. "Our rules reside in our minds and are passed down from the original members."

She placed the last of the burning embers on a plate and grabbed Luke's right hand to hold it still while she delicately sliced a shallow wound into his middle finger. Instead of pulling his hand away, his body seemed to stiffen. She didn't let go until crimson drops fell onto the remaining ashes in the plate, symbolizing his bond to the spoken words. Then she let go of him; elation came over her as his initiation made her feel closer to him.

Tony erupted. "Woo-hoo! You're in, Fighter. You're in!"

Luke laughed as he grabbed the bandage Sophia handed him. A popping sound came from behind the bar as Sammy opened a bottle of champagne.

"Did you think you were going to lose a finger?" Sophia asked.

"The thought crossed my mind, but I figured I'd still be mostly functional without my middle finger."

"That's where you're wrong, Fighter." Sammy laughed as he handed him a glass of champagne. "That's the one you'll need the most around here."

"Are you afraid of anything?" Sophia asked.

Luke's eyes met hers. "I'm sure I can think of some things."

"We should celebrate," Tony said. "How about a weekend with guys on the Las Vegas strip to let loose?"

"I don't know," Sophia said. "The last time we did that, it got way out of hand and the cops were called. That's the last thing we need."

"Kid, that bonehead, thought it'd be fun to have a jousting tournament on the rooftop of that old Showtime Hotel," Sammy explained. "When one of the lances went flying down off the roof and stabbed an empty tour bus, the cops were called in to shut us down."

"I can keep an eye on him," Luke said.

"Oh, I'm sure he'd love that," Sophia said. "Our newest member has to babysit him."

"He'll come around," Sammy said. "Maybe we'll put Luke and Kid together on the same projects. Luke will rub off on him and he'll have no choice but to wise up."

"Maybe," Luke said. "Or maybe he'll shoot me in my sleep."

Sammy shrugged. "That's also entirely possible. I'll tell you what, instead of wondering how he feels about it, we'll ask Kid tonight at your celebratory dinner. How does that sound?"

Luke smiled sheepishly. "I feel so special."

"You've earned it," Tony said. "I've got to put on a fresh coat of self-tanner. I'll meet you guys there."

"Are you serious?" Sammy asked.

"Dead serious." Tony gave him his megawatt smile as he made his way up the stairs.

****

Later that night at Isabella's restaurant, Luke barely heard his crew members tell war stories over the constant clanging of dishware and harried busboys working the tables around them. His mouth watered at the smell of fresh basil and pasta sauce permeating the air.

When was the last time he had a fancy meal at a restaurant? It had to have been when he'd first started bringing in the drug money. And, boy, did he really screw that up. Not used to having large quantities of cash, he'd gone on a spending spree that led to his ultimate demise. He'd become sloppy, returning to the same car dealership with large sums of cash to buy another of the newest hot rods. In doing so, they'd become suspicious and led the Feds right to him—not his smartest move. Lately, he wondered if he had secretly wanted to get caught. The pressure of hiding out and lying to everyone had probably become too much—not unlike his current situation.

Glancing to his right where Sophia sat in between Tony, Sammy and Francesca, Sammy's wife, Luke studied Sophia's silken black hair, curled at the ends into ringlets. She wore large gold earrings in the shape of circles, and her lips were a shock of red, like ripe summer strawberries. The sudden regret he had in trying to push her away threatened to eat him alive.

"Mr. Morello," a waiter dressed in a tuxedo said as he approached Sammy, "so nice to see you and Francesca tonight."

"I hope the sauce is fresh tonight, Gio," Francesca said, staring up at him through her thick-lensed glasses.

"The pasta is always fresh every day, my lady."

She wagged her pointer finger at him. "That's not what I heard. People are saying lately it tastes like it came from a jar."

"Francesca, come on," Sammy chastised her. "There's no way the pasta is not fresh."

She turned to Sammy. "That's what I heard from Caterina."

"The two of you talk too much. Come on, you're insulting the guy."

Francesca retreated. "All right, all right."

"Gio, we're celebrating tonight," Sammy said. "Bring us your best bottle of red and keep it coming."

"Bravo, Mr. Morello, right away." Then he nodded toward Sophia in a gesture of respect to the boss. "It's a pleasure to have you with us tonight."

"And bring those goat cheese crostinis that I like," Sammy added.

"Right away, sir."

On Luke's left, Kid sat with a scowl on his face— no doubt annoyed by Luke's rise in the ranks.

"Glad you could make it," Luke told him.

Kid shot him the death stare.

"Where were you?" Sammy asked.

Kid shrugged. "What do you mean? You know where I am. I'm always working like I'm supposed to be."

"You know the rules." Sammy gestured in Luke's direction. "You didn't come to his initiation."

"You were missed," Sophia added. "We were disappointed you didn't make the effort to show up."

"My stomach hurt," he said, grabbing the skin of his abdomen. "I couldn't make it. Too many spicy burritos."

"Kid, I don't care if your butt explodes, you have to come when someone is initiated to the group," Sammy said, tapping his finger into the white tablecloth.

"It's all right," Luke said. "He's here now."

He was trying to lighten the mood, but he could feel Sophia's eyes boring into him. Maybe he'd overstepped a bit, but he was part of the crew now and defending Kid might work in his favor.

Sammy cleared his throat as a flurry of waiters came around the table, setting down wine glasses in front of each crew member. Gio worked the corkscrew into the bottle with the ease of someone who'd done it a million times.

"Reminds me of the time Rocco told me I was becoming a made man," Tony explained, "and when I showed up for the ceremony, Sammy's face was white as a ghost. Then he walked out with no explanation, missing the entire event."

"That's not the same thing," Sammy said, swirling the wine Gio had poured and taking a sip. "This is good, Gio."

"Glad you like it," he said, going around to pour the wine for the others.

Luke couldn't help noticing Sammy seemed like the actual boss of this crew while Sophia was their unwilling puppet.

"I had emergency business to attend to," Sammy explained. "Nothing I can talk about here."

"Or was it spicy burritos?" Tony laughed.

"Ah, come on," Sammy said. "You guys have it really easy. When I was coming up, Rocco was testing me to my breaking point and then he went even further."

"We know. We know," Tony said. "You've told the story a million times."

Sammy swirled the wine in his glass, sticking his nose in the glass for a long whiff. Then he took a sip. "Luke hasn't heard it." He turned to Luke. "Sophia's been very kind to you. Back in my day, we had to whack somebody to prove our loyalty."

"Sammy!" Francesca chastised him. "Can we not talk about that here?"

He spread his arms wide. "Listen, these are my people."

"She's right, Sammy," Tony said. "A couple drinks, and you think you're invincible."

"I assume it wasn't anyone you were friends with?" Luke asked.

"Nah, it was always an enemy or someone trying to

mess up our business," Sammy said.

"That's a relief," Luke said just as Gio placed a tray of goat cheese crostinis on the table in front of Sammy.

"Just in time, Gio," Sammy said. "I was going to reach over this table and smack that fake tan off of Tony's face."

Gio laughed. "Ah, come on. We don't want that. It looks so good on him."

"I never understood why Tony never found himself a good wife. Such a good-looking guy," Francesca interjected.

"Don't look at my wife," Sammy quipped at Tony.

"Listen, when I see true beauty"—Tony made a chef's kiss gesture toward Francesca—"no one else can pull me away."

Francesca giggled into her wine glass.

"The point is," Sammy said, turning back to Luke, "Rocco was a force to reckon with. I learned a lot early on when I was still a teenager sneaking out to run errands for him. My parents wanted to kill me themselves for associating with his crew but when they saw the money coming in, they turned a blind eye." He popped a crostini in his mouth, crunching down loudly as crumbs fell onto his checkered silk tie.

Luke couldn't help relating to Sammy's story. His family had also fallen on hard times—their dreams crushed under the weight of financial ruin. Going the illegal route was the only way to save them and that's what he did to give them a better life. He hated to admit it, but he had a lot in common with these guys, making it more difficult for him to implicate them. But the difference was the sworn oath he'd just taken meant nothing. He would rat on them before being sent to prison for the rest of his life.

"Speaking of Rocco," Sophia chimed in, "he sent over a video message for Luke. One of his guys recorded for him on the inside. She pushed her phone on the table toward Luke.

"That's an honor," Tony said. "Must've been tricky to get that recording done."

"He's very resourceful," Sophia replied.

Luke grabbed the phone. He recognized Rocco's face on the screen from the framed photos in Sophia's living room. Although, in those photos he appeared healthier and happier. In this version his cheeks were gaunt, his dark hair had white patches throughout it and the circles under his eyes were sunken. The only part of him that resembled Sophia were those dark blue eyes. The same ones that haunted him when he laid his head on his pillow every night.

Pressing play on the screen, he wondered if the recording device would pick up the message.

"This is for Luke Daniels," Rocco began on the screen.

His voice sounded surprisingly soft.

"Congratulations on becoming part of the Costa Crew. Sophia has told me about your accomplishments and quick rise up the ranks. She's told me how you've stepped up when her life or other member's lives were in danger and she's even described you as fearless, loyal but not careless. Those are all the traits we want for our members."

Luke loosened his grip on the phone as his hands began to sweat. Little did Rocco know about the treachery. The extent of which rivaled his worst nightmares. A quick glance around the table showed the reverence at which the members held their leader, except for Kid. His cheeks burned the color red, likely from the anger he held inside of being passed over for a random guy off the street.

"Keep up the good work," Rocco's message continued. But then his eyes narrowed as he stared into the camera, the killer replacing the politician. "And remember, I might be behind concrete walls now, but one misstep and I will find you, like a hawk hunts a rat." A second later, the cold ice left his stare. "Don't ever forget that."

****

"Look at this guy." Troy Wilson stood up in the booth of the Desert Oasis Diner with a big smile on his face.

Luke looked around the diner. "You're disturbing the other two people having breakfast this morning."

"I'm fine with that. Have a seat. You want a steak? You can have anything you want."

Luke smirked as he sat in the booth across from Troy. "I did something right for once."

Troy leaned toward him. "Are you kidding? Not only did you become a member of the Costa Crew, but you were able to record the whole thing. No one has ever done that. We had suspicions about what goes on during an initiation ceremony but nothing concrete."

Luke struggled with Troy's celebratory feelings. It's true he'd completely succeeded in infiltrating the Costa Crew—a near impossible task—but the lies he'd told to get there filled him with disgust. "I'm glad you're happy."

Troy studied Luke's face. "Oh, come on. You're not having second thoughts, are you? Now that you've gotten this far. Don't you realize you're going to be part of every important conversation they have from now on? It won't be little bits and pieces like before. We're going to get information that will finally bring the organization down."

Luke nodded. "I get it. I get it. I know what it means." He stayed quiet. The more he spoke about this topic the more likely Troy would get suspicious and pull him out.

"Listen, *Fighter*, if you're sleeping with the enemy, you'd better tell me now—"

"I'm not. I already told you I'm not on their side." Luke scanned Troy's stern facial expression. "Aren't there ever any gray areas with you?"

"If you're asking me if I've ever felt bad about an arrest, the answer is yes."

"Really? *You've* made mistakes?"

"I lost an informant once."

Luke's smirk faded.

"The most dangerous part of this process is when we come out of nowhere to arrest the criminals, but we also have to protect our informant. I had a guy who'd been in the trenches for a very long time. Collecting the surveillance had been slow. When we finally got what we needed, we went in for the arrest but, boy, were those mafia members pissed when we burst out of nowhere. Our informant got caught in the crossfire and didn't make it out alive. You could say we do more harm than good, but the FBI will never see it that way. So, to answer your question, are there gray areas? Yes, but we'll always be on the right side of the law, and I suggest you stick with me if you want to beat the rap."

"I can't say that's comforting but I'm encouraged by

the progress I've made. We're talking about people's lives here."

"And there will be losers in this game," Troy said. "There's nothing you can do about that. Not even if they think you're their new best buddy or if you think they care about you."

"Sometimes, I don't feel like I'm winning."

"Get used to it. Don't get sucked in. If you need me to remind you from time to time why you are doing this, I can do that. It's not easy but I know you can get to the end. You've got to hang in there." Troy leaned in closer to Luke. "So, tell me, how does it feel to be a member of the Costa Clan?"

"I feel like a fraud."

Troy narrowed his eyes. "It's not like you are a schoolteacher being forced into the mafia. You're a convicted criminal."

"I'm nothing like them." His nostrils flared. "My first thought isn't to kill people to keep them quiet or to protect one's honor. I may be a criminal, but I worked alone, and I never killed anyone. You can't just take anyone off the street and turn them into a mobster. That's something they learn how to be from an early age. I will never fully understand them."

He thought about Sophia's desire to be something else but how she struggled to let go of what had been ingrained in her from the beginning. He wondered if she could ever truly let go of being a mob boss.

"Whatever you've been doing is good enough. They clearly are buying it and that's all we ask of you. When you come out of this you can go back to being Luke Daniels, but you'll be better off knowing you were part of a mafia shakedown. I can't think of a better deal than that."

Luke wanted to believe him but all he heard were words that had very little meaning to him. He did not share Troy's agenda, but he did want to stay out of jail. And so, for now he would pretend to be a member of the Costa Clan. "I'm not that hungry." He stood up to leave. "Are we done here?"

"Leaving so soon? I've offered you steak. The offer ends today."

Luke watched the waitress take a pile of soggy fries over to the only other occupied table. "Tempting, but I've got to pack."

Troy's eyebrow shot up. "Pack? Should I arrest you now for defecting from the FBI?"

"I'm not running away. The crew is going on a trip to Las Vegas for a bit of. . .bonding as they've called it."

"I see. Sounds like nothing I can use on tape. Drinking, gambling, and girls won't amount to anything useful, but maybe you can bring up your new business interests with them."

Luke nodded. "We'll see." He turned to leave.

"Oh, and Luke?"

He turned his head back toward Troy.

"Watch your back. I hear there's a hitman looking for your new boss."

"Can't your people take care of it?"

"We never influence the natural course of things, and we don't really care about the hitman. We're focusing on the bigger picture. Got it?"

Luke nodded. "I understand completely. What you're saying is, I'm on my own."

Chapter Fourteen

Cigar smoke filled Luke's nostrils as he entered the penthouse suite the crew had rented out on the Las Vegas strip for their weekend of bonding. He'd stayed on the strip before but never thought to rent out a massive room for himself during his more prosperous times. Over four thousand square feet of luxurious furnishings assaulted his senses. Dozens of people milled around, enjoying the game tables set up around the suite but what stopped him in his tracks was the infinity pool along the far window with a view of the strip below. Girls in bikinis splashed and danced to loud music blasting through the speakers, making him feel like he was on a movie set, except no one was going to yell *cut*.

"Hey, Fighter. You made it." Sammy came over and hugged him. "Can you believe all this?"

Luke shook his head. "No, I pictured us hanging out in some dive bar, maybe doing some gambling, but never this."

"See, you made the right decision to join us— always the best for the crew. Why don't you go grab a drink over by the bar? I'm heading over to the poker table. Enjoy yourself for a bit. I've got a little surprise for you later." Sammy slapped Luke's shoulder and went toward a game table.

Luke shook his head, not knowing what that meant and coming from Sammy, it could mean trouble.

Weaving by game tables, Luke noticed Sophia by the bar—a dark beauty among thugs, pulling him in toward her like a siren he couldn't resist.

Her smile grabbed him by the throat as he approached her at the bar. "This is nuts."

She sipped her martini, leaving a red lipstick stain on the rim. "Sometimes I feel like a bird in a cage surrounded by feral cats. I needed a distraction for the boys."

"I get that." Luke turned to the bartender. "Can I get two tequila shots, please?" After the bartender poured the two shots, Luke handed one to Sophia as she placed her martini glass on the bar. "Sometimes you have to let your hair down. Cheers." He threw back the shot and signaled for another one.

Sophia took her shot without cringing. "How does it feel to be a member?"

"Should I feel different?" Luke took the second shot, feeling the burn down his throat.

"Well, *I* had a feeling about you, and I was right."

"Are you sure? I could be the enemy," he said, aware of his loosened tongue. It also didn't hurt that he had no plans on wearing the recording device this weekend.

"You'd be a lousy one since you've already missed so many opportunities to clip the boss." She leaned in closer to his ear. "It's loud in here. There's a terrace leading out of the master that's supposed to have amazing views of the strip. You want to go check it out?"

"Sounds good to me," he said, following her but also acutely aware that he was leading her on.

As they walked outside, the night sky pulsed with multicolored neon lights. The sound of music and chatter made its way all the way up from the street to the penthouse.

"Wow. You were right. This view is crazy," he said as he watched the glowing lights land on her perfect skin. Maybe for once he could act on how he felt and not have it completely blow up in his face.

"I have great memories here," she said, smiling at the view. "My dad used to bring my brother and I here and we'd stay in the coolest hotels in those days. I remember my bedroom had a giant slide that spit me out onto the bed when I was ready to go to sleep."

Luke smiled. "That does sound cool."

"He tried to make everything pleasant for us even if he'd just whacked someone an hour before dinner. We never caught on. Mom would tell us he was working late in the pizza shops our family owned and we had no reason not to believe her. Until the day I woke up on a cold January morning to find Mom crying over her coffee cup. Dad had been murdered by a rival member in an attempt to take over his crew."

"Geez, how old were you?"

"Eleven. That's when we learned the truth. My uncle fought them hard and took over the crew until my brother was old enough. That's also when I realized there was no getting out. I was born into something, and the only way out was my death."

His jaw clenched at the unfairness of it all. "You could go to the police."

She glared at him. "Yeah, right. No one does that."

"I bet you've thought about it."

"Bite your tongue," she said, looking around to make sure no one heard them. "I am the boss. If someone overheard, they could spread rumors and then I'm dead."

"Oh, come on." He put his arm around her waist,

drawing her closer. "You can tell me. Doesn't freedom from all the responsibilities sound amazing?"

Her cheeks blushed. "Maybe I'd like to try a life without bandits and not have to worry about my every move. But where would I go? And who would look out for you?"

He stared into her dark blue eyes, wondering how he'd gotten into this mess. He'd never been so confused about what he wanted. Logically, he needed to focus on the goal of staying out of jail, but he couldn't help himself. She was special, possibly worth risking everything. Maybe Troy would agree she was a pawn in this game and let her off easy. Maybe they could be free together. "What if I said I would come with you?"

She paused, looking stunned by his revelation. Then she narrowed her eyes. "I thought you wanted to cool things off between us. You seem to be suffering some kind of identity crisis."

He nodded. "You couldn't be more right about that and I'm sorry I'm putting out mixed signals. I can't seem to listen to my own advice around you."

"Well, I would definitely go somewhere with you. But there would probably be backlash for abandoning my crew and it wouldn't end well—best to stay put than wind up dead."

"For tonight, I want to pretend we could get away with it." He let the tequila remove whatever was left of his inhibitions, pulled her in closer and gave her one soft but short kiss. By a long shot, her lips were the plushest he'd ever kissed. It'd been a while, too, since he pursued anyone in his underground type of lifestyle. Mostly because he didn't want to drag anyone into danger, but he couldn't deny he'd been drawn to Sophia since the first time he'd laid eyes on her and not doing something about it had been difficult—basically impossible. And he knew he wanted more.

"And I think you like me, too."

She laughed as she playfully straightened his shirt collar. "I can't confirm or deny."

"Seems pretty obvious to me," he said, leaning in for another kiss, a deeper one this time—

"There you are, Fighter." Tony's booming voice pulled them apart as he walked toward them with a huge smile. "Boy, does Sammy have a surprise for you."

Luke cleared his throat, annoyed with the intrusion but willing to act as if Tony didn't see anything. "I bet. What is it? A trophy? A new car?"

"Even better. He got you a fight in an actual arena."

"He did what? That's impossible. I'm not even qualified to fight in an arena." Then he remembered who he was dealing with and how most things could be bought or coerced if needed.

"Come on! We've got to go," he barked, ushering them inside. "Fighter, you more than anyone should know by now, with the Costa Crew, anything is possible."

****

"This is it?" Luke complained while standing outside of the small run-down arena as the crew got out of their cars.

"What do you mean?" Sammy asked. "What do you want from me? In its day this place was the go-to spot. It needs a little help but there's a lot of history there. Haven't you heard of the great Jessie 'Southpaw' Santana?"

"No."

"He used to confuse his opponents with his right-sided stance. Man, he had some of the greatest boxing tactics born out of this very arena." He turned toward Luke. "You better learn a thing or two about the world of boxing if you're going to call yourself a fighter."

"You guys created this monster." He put his hand to his chest. "Not me. Are people still allowed in there?" Luke asked, analyzing the crumbling facade.

Sammy's one eye glared at him. "I'm sure it will stay up long enough for this fight. Come on, let's meet your opponent and try to be a little grateful."

"I'm grateful. I'm grateful. When you said arena, I was thinking of something else."

"Who do you think you are? A pop star? You do get an audience this time. I've got people lined up around the back ready to come in and pay to see you fight. This is the best I could do."

"It's wonderful, Sammy," Sophia added. "This could really be a lucrative move toward expanding our businesses." She turned toward Luke. "Don't you agree?"

He nodded. "Getting my face bashed in on a regular basis sounds like a great idea for me."

She cocked her head. "But you're so talented. It's a no-brainer."

"That's exactly right. I'll have no brain left from all the repeated punches to my head."

She laughed, pulling him into the entrance. "You'll be great."

"Who am I fighting this time?" Luke asked, turning to Sammy. "A world champion gold medalist?"

"Even if I *could* get that guy, I have no doubt you'd beat him." Sammy slapped Luke's back and then pointed to a duffel bag by the ring. "We believe in you so much that we all chipped in and got you some new gear. Take a look inside."

"You're kidding?" Luke walked over and unzipped the bag, pulling out a brand-new pair of red boxing gloves. Luke whistled. "These are nice."

"There's more in here. Check it out," Tony said, joining the group from outside.

Luke reached in and pulled out a black satin ring robe. Turning it around to see the back, the name *Fighter* was there in big bold red letters. "Wow. You guys really went there."

"Only the best for you," Sammy said. "We know you have talent, and we want you to take this seriously."

"You guys are the best." Luke hugged both Sammy and Tony. "I've never had anyone care this much about me. I'm honored." He looked down, genuinely overcome with emotion. The conflict in his heart made him feel terrible for deceiving them. He hadn't expected the camaraderie between them to grow as fast as it had over the last few weeks or to experience kindness and generosity from mobsters. It killed him that this boxing gig would be short-lived. "Did Kid chip in too?"

Sammy chuckled. "He'll be here soon. We all contributed, remember that."

"When do I meet the brute I'm going to take down?"

A loud bang made Luke jump. "What's that?" He looked toward the side entrance. Kid had pushed the door open, slamming it against the opposite wall.

"Run! The cops are coming!" Kid yelled and gestured for them to follow him. "My car is out this way."

Luke grabbed the duffel bag and Sophia's hand as

they ran toward the side door while the rest of the crew followed behind. They quickly piled into Kid's SUV. He sped out before the cops could see them.

Swerving around cars, Kid pushed on the gas enough to put quite a bit of distance between them and the arena.

"What was that about?" Sammy asked once Kid had slowed down.

"I was pulling up when I saw cop cars coming up from behind me. So, I decided to pull up on the side of the building."

"Good thinking, Kid," Sammy said.

"Or did you tip them off?" Luke asked.

Kid looked at Luke's reflection in the rearview mirror. "Are you serious? You can't say that?"

"Can't I?" He knew Kid couldn't say much since he was lower ranked. "How did the cops know where to find us? Sounds like someone told them there was an unlicensed fight going on in a condemned building."

"Ah, come on, Fighter," Sammy said. "He wouldn't do that."

"Yeah, that doesn't even make sense. Why would I warn you if I wanted you to get arrested?" Kid asked.

Luke's mind flashed back to the humiliating moment he stripped his clothes off in front of the entire crew and Sophia. "Doesn't feel good to be questioned, does it?"

The car fell silent.

"I didn't tip them off," Kid said in a low voice. "I would be sabotaging myself."

"Well, maybe you're all right with that as long as I don't get what I want. You don't want to see me succeed. You're jealous the guys went to all this effort for me.

You hate that I can fight and you can't." Luke spat.

Kid swerved into an alley and hit the brakes. "Let's go!" he yelled as he jumped out of the car and walked a few feet ahead, facing the car. "Let's see who can fight. Come on!"

Luke rolled his eyes. "Is he serious?"

"Maybe you should whip his butt. That might shut him up for once," Sammy said. "You can't stay in the car. You've got to do something."

"Let him have a few hits," Tony chimed in. "It'll make him feel better and then we can move on."

Luke shot him an annoyed look but then got out of the car in no particular hurry.

Kid waited for him, bouncing around in a ready position.

But Luke towered over him. "Come on. Let's see what you've got." He gestured for Kid to start.

Kid wasted no time. He barreled forward and swung a right uppercut.

Luke barely reacted. A punch to the face stings but not much if you don't know what you're doing. "Happy? Can we go now? I'm getting kind of hungry."

Kid's face scrunched up in anger. He launched forward, landing a right and a left hook one after the other, sending Luke stumbling backward. Catching himself before he went down, Luke leaped toward Kid with a hard right to the cheek. It only took one to bring him down.

Sammy came out of the car, running toward them. "That's enough. You both made your points. We need to get out of here before someone sees and calls the cops for a second time." He helped pull Kid off the floor and back into the car.

"I'm fine. I can drive," Kid said, rubbing his cheek.

"Are you sure?" Sammy asked.

"Yeah, it's fine. I was about to get back up and keep going if you hadn't stopped me," Kid said.

"Let's go already. It isn't safe around here," Sophia warned.

Kid pulled out of the alley and drove away from the arena as no one dared say another word.

"Isn't that interesting?" Tony asked, finally breaking the silence.

"Isn't *what* interesting?" Sammy replied.

"The cops shut down our fight today, but we got to see one anyway."

"It certainly would've ended the same way," Sammy said. "But we would've made some money at the arena."

"It's not always about money," Luke said. Lord knows he wouldn't be in this mess had he not cared about the piles of money he was making illegally.

"No, it's about loyalty," Sammy said.

Internally, Luke cringed.

"And a perfectly crispy cannoli," Tony said.

Sophia giggled. "Let's get some dinner. I know a place with the best vodka sauce on the Las Vegas strip."

"What's it called?" Tony asked.

"*Famiglia.*"

Chapter Fifteen

Sophia stared at the orange glow on the horizon as she rode a tawny-blonde horse through a dusty canyon outside the Las Vegas city limits. Her dad used to take her and her brother on the same exact trail any time he needed a break from the craziness. She loved those trips and, boy, did she understand why he needed to get away. Plus, she also wanted a break from the Luke drama. The way they openly showed their affection for each other could get them in trouble. Had she tried to stop it? Not really. He represented the life she never knew.

Luke could be her ticket to freedom or…death.

"Couldn't we have gone to a spa?" Tony, atop a palomino behind her, yelled.

She turned to look at him. Even though she'd sprung this horse-riding trip on him at the last minute, she couldn't help but chuckle at his insistence on wearing his gray suit. The way he clutched the reins out of terror also didn't help her keep a straight face.

"Spa? Look at that sunset. Don't you like breathing in the fresh air and getting some exercise away from all the noise?"

"Fresh air?" he said, patting the horse's neck. "All I smell is Ghost's last dump."

Sophia heard Duke Baker, their tour guide, snicker. "Not the outdoor type, Tony?" Duke asked, spitting into the ground and then adjusting his cowboy hat.

"If going outside to get into your car counts as being outdoors. I don't see why anyone would want this type of abuse on the body. I prefer something gentler."

"Like joining a book club?" Duke's shoulders rocked with his raspy laugh.

"Those clubs can be vicious. Ask my Nonna Maria," Tony replied.

Sophia chuckled. Little did Duke know, Tony could slit his throat before his horse took its next step and be ready to have bloody steak for dinner without batting an eye. She'd seen it with her own eyes.

Tony slowed his horse down, allowing them to have a private conversation.

She got the hint and fell in line with Tony's pace.

"Sophia, the boyfriend didn't want to come?" Tony asked.

Her stomach clenched. "Boyfriend?"

"Yeah, you know, Luke."

"You're funny," she said, dismissing his comment. "I didn't ask him if he wanted to come along."

"You two have a fight?"

Sophia smiled. Tony sounded just like her dad. If she closed her eyes, she could picture him asking her the same questions. "He's not my boyfriend."

"No? Sure seemed like something was going on the couple of times I ran into you two when you were alone."

"Maybe you wanted to see something that wasn't there."

"Look, I like the guy. If I were angry about this, his head would already be buried somewhere in the desert. I think it's a nice distraction for you but be careful. Some of the other guys may not agree with it. They'll think he got to where he is because of you and that's not good for either of you."

"Luke has proven himself time after time to be worthy of his position. I'm glad you like him, but I think you're reading into this too much. I'll admit to mild flirting and nothing more. Besides, if he were here, I would be too distracted to witness your attempt to ride a horse."

"I think I'm doing a great job for my first time riding a horse. Enjoy the laughs now because when we get back, we really need to get back to business. Like I said, I like Luke. He's a nice addition to the team but to keep everyone from getting suspicious of his role, we need to see what he can actually do for us."

Sophia bit the insides of her cheeks. In her cloud-filled mind, she assumed Luke would be great for their business, but she'd taken a gamble and didn't know for sure. She realized it was unusual for a prospective member to seek them out. Usually, the crew chooses the new recruits. But Luke came to Lucky Guess that day on a mission. She had to believe he'd be a great addition.

"Agreed. He's the one who came to us. I'm sure he's eager to get started."

"All right, folks"—Duke pointed up ahead—"that right there is the crystal cave. Formed from limestone millions of years ago, the crystals inside were created from a process called nucleation."

"Nucle—what?" Tony asked.

Sophia glared at him.

"I can't say I'm not surprised you ditched science class in grade school," Duke said with a roll of his eyes.

"I had other *projects* going on at the time."

"I bet. Anyway, molecules from a liquid solution became arranged or stuck together in a pattern that formed the crystals that you see today."

Tony yawned.

Duke stared at him. "Am I boring you?"

"Not at all. Last night when Sophia told me about this tour, I was so excited I couldn't sleep."

"Tony!" Sophia chastised him.

"Uh-huh." Duke ignored him as he forged ahead. "We can go inside and take a peek." He pointed at Tony. "Since you don't care for nature, you can stay here and make sure the horses don't run off."

Tony jumped off his horse and stumbled forward a few feet. "Fine with me. I've already got horse dung on my loafers. I don't need rocks in my shoes as well."

Sophia and Duke lowered themselves off their horses. "We won't be long," she said. "I never got a chance to go as a kid. Dad thought it was too dangerous—which seems strange coming from him."

"He was right, it is dangerous," Tony said. "Shouldn't you be wearing helmets? Shiny or not, those rocks can fall on your head and knock you out."

"Nah," Duke said as they walked to the cave entrance. "Those rocks are stuck on tight. It's really safe."

"Dang, I was hoping to bring some crystals home," Sophia said.

"That's why I brought this," Duke said, showing her the small pickaxe he'd been carrying on his tool belt.

"Splendid," she replied.

"You didn't tell me you were bringing weapons. Seems unfair if Sophia didn't bring any," Tony yelled.

Sophia turned around. "Who says I didn't?" Then she walked onward to the cave.

Inside the mouth of the cave, Duke turned on his

flashlight and pointed the light down the dark passage in front of them. "We'll need to go down a few yards to get to the crystals. I'll lead with the light."

She stared into the darkness, wondering what she had gotten herself into. Her breath came a little faster as she followed Duke into the abyss. What she had told Tony wasn't a lie. She'd hidden a small pistol in the pocket of her khaki cargo pants as a precaution. But her trip out to ride horses hadn't raised any eyebrows so far. Her sneakers crunched over the rocky ground as she tried not to trip over the larger boulders.

"Seems a bit rockier here than you had explained earlier," she said, trying to follow the beam of light coming from his flashlight.

He didn't reply. Her heart thumped in her ears. Everything in her body was telling her to turn around and run. She looked up at the ceiling. Her eyes struggled to discern anything, but nothing sparkled down at her.

"When do the crystals show up?"

He didn't turn back. "Just a little further now and we'll see an entire room full of them."

She breathed a little easier with that response. Maybe she'd been anxious for no reason. "That sounds lovely."

A minute passed before she noticed Duke begin to slow down. Ahead, she saw no opening leading up to the promised room with crystals. Her hands slid toward the pocket with the gun. Before she could think about pulling the pistol out, Duke turned around, holding the pickaxe out in his right hand.

"I have a confession," he said.

She cocked her head at him.

He chuckled. "I'm sorry to inform you but there's

no crystal room. I'm not really a horse trail guide and somebody close to you wants you dead."

Sophia's heart stopped. The hitman. She'd spent the last hour following a hitman into the middle of nowhere deep into a cave where no one would be able to help her. She wanted to grab that gun in her pocket but also didn't want to make any sudden moves for fear he would just pounce on her with the pickaxe.

Duke's expression shifted. The cold stare in his eyes made her spine tingle. He meant business. He lunged at her with the pickaxe. She ducked out of the way, giving her enough time to get the gun out of her cargo pants pocket. Her awkward handling of the gun didn't give her enough time to point it at him but instead she whacked it at his temple as he tried a second attempt with the axe. The impact of the gun to his head sent him and the gun to the floor. She wasted no time waiting around for his next move.

As she barreled down the darkness without a flashlight, her lungs burned as she pumped her legs harder than ever before. Footsteps following behind forced her to push even faster as he gained speed. His grunting noises echoed against the walls down the passage that seemed to never end. At the moment she thought she might give up and let him win, the light from the cave entrance came into view. Screams erupted from her throat as she burst through the entrance and tumbled to the ground. Shots rang out, and Duke dropped, face-first, into the dirt.

Tony rushed toward her as he put his gun back in its holster. "Are you hurt?" He put his hand out to help her up.

She pulled herself up. "No, I should've known better

than to go into a dark cave with some stranger."

"I'm the one who let you go. It's my fault. My job is to keep this from happening." He spit at Duke's body. "Who is this guy anyway?"

Sophia paused for a moment. "He said someone close to me wanted me dead."

Tony's eyes opened wide. "Christ, another hired hitman?"

"Someone close to me...within our group?"

Tony shook his head. "Can't be. I can't think of one person who's unhappy—"

"What about Kid? He's unhappy about Luke and all his success."

His face scrunched up. "Kid? I find that hard to believe and what does that have to do with you?"

"I made Luke a member and not Kid. That would piss me off if I were him." She shrugged her shoulders. "Or what about Carmine again?"

Tony scanned the darkening sky. "I doubt it. I think Carmine's beef has been taken care of."

She shook her head. "He still hates me. I don't think that issue is squashed."

Tony took out his cellular phone and called some of the guys out to help with the cleanup and disposal. Then he put his phone back in his pocket. "I have an idea." He held up his pointer finger. "Hear me out. Let's make Kid a member of the crew."

Sophia looked at him like he had two heads. "Kid? You want Kid to be a member?"

"If it would stop the targets, then yes. It's the only way to rule him out as the instigator of these attacks."

She couldn't believe her ears and yet at the same time recognized it did make sense. "If we do this and find out it was him all along, are you going to be able to sleep at night knowing we made Kid a member even though he was trying to have me killed?"

He scanned her face. "It's a risk I'm willing to take to find out the truth. Plus, I know you can handle yourself. You've taken some punches and given some back and you know we're not exactly making baby food out here. These aren't nice people. They're murderers. To answer your question, I think you can take him if needed but hopefully, it won't come to that."

"And what if it's not Kid? What if it's someone else we haven't looked at close enough?" she asked.

"If it's not Kid, we'll have to scrutinize all the other possible members and their contacts who may have shown any disrespect or seem disgruntled toward you."

She smirked. "That's a long list."

"And we'll go through each and every one to find him, I promise."

****

Jaw clenched, Luke scanned the scrapes on Sophia's hands as she prepared to slice into Kid's finger for his initiation into the crew. He'd not been there to cut Duke's throat for trying to kill her; now he had to watch as they brought Kid in as a member despite his total incompetence and bad attitude.

As she pierced Kid's finger, Luke hoped she'd chop the whole finger off. Instead, when the deed was done and Kid only received a scrape, the room erupted in celebration, and Luke walked away looking to pour himself a drink. A shot of tequila at Sophia's bar was the best he could find on demand. The first one burned his throat mercilessly. Enjoying the pain, he took another one, hoping it would distract him from reality.

"You know why we did this, right?" Sophia said, coming up behind him.

He shook his head. "It's bad news."

"I don't think so." She lowered her voice. "If the hits on my life stop, then we know it was him and he will be dealt with immediately. If not, at least the tension between you two will stop—seems like a win-win situation."

"Kid is not going to be a good addition to the group. We're going to be cleaning up his screw-ups, which won't look good to our customers. It's also a huge distraction in looking for the real hitman."

She breathed in. "Well, it's done. I think we should stop worrying about him and focus on your next venture." She put her arms around his waist. "This should be an exciting time for you."

He pulled her arms apart. "You shouldn't be so obvious about us—especially now that anyone can join the group."

She stepped back but didn't lose her smile. "Can you look at me?"

He reluctantly turned around, not wanting to say anything cruel to her face.

"First of all, *you* kissed me in Las Vegas, remember?" She wagged her pointer finger at him. "Or was that the tequila talking?"

"Of course I remember."

"You seem to have a habit of kissing me and then telling me we need to cool it."

He snorted, staring at the floor. "True. Maybe you should refuse my advances."

She lifted his chin, meeting his gaze. "Impossible. I simply cannot resist you."

His chest tightened. This was all his fault. "If I were you, I would try harder."

She smiled, dismissing his advice. "I've set your business up inside Luigi's pizza shop just off the strip. There, you can work on getting your contacts in order and start setting up your online shop—"

"I know how it works," he snapped. "I have a lot of experience, remember?" He barked at her knowing he'd slipped the recording device into his sock to record Kid's initiation but not expecting Sophia to incriminate herself or display any public affection around the crew.

She stared at him.

The hurt in her eyes stung his soul. "I'm grateful for all that you've done for me. I am," he said—then backtracked. "I can't wait to get started but I'm worried we're bringing your enemies even closer to you." It wasn't untrue, but it wasn't the whole truth either.

"I'm fine." She grinned, diffusing the tension. "I've been through a lot worse than this. There's nothing to be worried about. As long as you keep me honest among my men by providing the income you said you would, then they won't question a thing. If you feel like you can't do that, better let me know sooner than later."

A lump formed in his throat. She may be messing with him, but he knew the truth. None of her plans would ever pan out and all of it would eventually come to an end. There would be no income provided by him. And as soon as the Feds had enough on tape that he provided them, they would strike, and all of this would be over. For now, he'd play the part and hope that Troy would go easy on her. "I'll provide what you need. Don't worry about that," he said in a low voice.

"Good." She eyed him up and down.

"There you are," Kid said, coming into the kitchen. "The guys were wondering if you two had left the party."

"I was making sure the tequila tastes right," Luke said.

"I bet," Kid replied with smiles he'd clearly been unable to produce before.

"Do you feel like you can stand to be around me now?" Luke said, with annoyance in his voice.

"I don't have a problem with you. In fact, I like you. When you stepped into Lucky Guess that night and told me you had just come out of prison, I knew I was going to like you."

Sophia eyed Luke. "You didn't tell us that."

He returned her glance without further explanation. Kid couldn't be trusted with his friendship. He'd done nothing but act like a pouty toddler. "You told me that night you had also recently gotten out of prison."

Kid laughed. "I said that to bond with you, like brothers and look at us now."

Luke stared at him. "Who are you really, Stefano?"

The smile left Kid's face. "I'm Stefano Ricci, member of the Costa Crew and loyal comrade to the organization long before you showed up out of nowhere with no affiliation to the crew."

"So that's your problem with me, huh? That I walked into a bar out of the blue and they made me a member? You don't think I worked for it? You don't think I put my life on the line for it? And then you go around accusing me of being a snitch."

Kid spread his arms out. "I was jealous, all right? Is that what you want to hear? I've spent most of my life willing to do anything to be a member of this crew. I walked away from my brother and the rest of my family to join this one. They wanted nothing to do with me after they found out who I was hanging around." His voice rose. "I should be rewarded for that kind of loyalty but instead I got passed over for some guy who clearly has a shady background. I should ask, who are *you* really, *Fighter*?"

"I'm your worst nightmare," Luke said without flinching. Then he cracked a smile, knowing he had to lose this standoff for now.

Sophia chuckled. "That was pretty cheesy. Kid, clearly your persistence has paid off. Let's go join the others in the living room to celebrate. Luke, if you can get past your worries, feel free to join."

He watched her sultry eyes flirt with him, feeling guilty about liking every second. "Of course I'm coming. This is an important event."

She nodded. "Great."

"And you should enjoy any party while you still can," Luke added.

She cocked her head. "Why? What's going to happen? Am I going somewhere?"

He nodded. "Yes, back in hiding."

Chapter Sixteen

Luke felt the weight of Troy's stone-faced stare across the booth at their usual diner spot early in the morning. The smell of burnt toast permeated the air while an elderly couple sat on the opposite side of the diner, eating scrambled eggs and grits. Having lost his appetite, Luke's stomach twisted in anticipation of this meeting, knowing he'd been playing both sides of the fence and some of it had been caught on tape.

"Have fun in Vegas?" Troy asked.

Luke kept his expression neutral. "It was all right."

"For your sake and mine, I'm glad you didn't wear the device that weekend. Based on the most recent recordings, it seems your relationships have evolved."

Play dumb. "How so?"

"I could be wrong, but it seems like you're protecting the boss—among other things."

Luke let out his breath. "You're well aware there's a hitman on the loose but you aren't willing to do anything about it. I can't just sit back and watch bad things happen."

"That's obstruction. In fact, that's exactly what I want you to do, nothing."

Luke shook his head. "I can't. I don't have it in me."

Troy shrugged. "All right. You want to keep racking up the charges? Any of them will stick." Troy picked up an overdone strip of bacon and popped it into his mouth.

"And you keep arguing with Stefano Ricci. He's clearly suspicious about your intentions."

"Wouldn't you be if a guy came out of nowhere and rose up faster than the other recruits who've been around longer?"

"Sure, but you're not making it any better by antagonizing him. Sometimes, I think you forget you are playing a role and that everything you say or do has consequences for this case. Think about that next time you want to flirt with the boss."

Luke squirmed in his seat. How can he make Troy understand what it's been like for him from day to day? He needed to keep him from focusing on his relationship with Sophia and instead acknowledge what he had accomplished until now. "Did you know Tony plays the piano? He's been playing since he was a child. On Monday nights he plays at Lucky Guess during happy hour."

Troy remained expressionless. "Tony Russo plays the piano for fun. All right, I might've heard that."

"Or that Sammy just had twin baby boy grandchildren born this week? And his wife, Francesca, has been in and out of the hospital for asthma."

"Sounds like a stressful household but no different than anyone else's," Troy said in a monotone voice.

"Sophia's mom tripped and fell outside of her house and broke her wrist the other day. She'll have to be in a cast for a few weeks."

"No, I wasn't aware. Should I send her some flowers?" Troy raised his voice.

Luke rolled his eyes. "The point is these are people who have lives just like me and you. I'm the one who has to get inside and listen to all their problems and be invested in them. I'm playing the game like you want me to but I'm also human. Haven't you heard the expression, keep your enemies closer?"

"Well, you should've been an actor instead of a career criminal. You would've won all the awards with your performance."

"You want me to get killed?" Luke's eyes narrowed. "I'm the one putting my life on the line every day. If they don't believe me, I'm dead." His voice rose. "And you're making jokes?"

Troy looked away, breaking the tension. "I'll take your word for it but the only way to get anything concrete is at the scene of the crime. We need you there making the transactions on behalf of the Costa Crew."

"I told you. I'm working on it. I can't help how good-looking I am, and the boss of the Costa Crew can't keep her hands off of me. Occupational hazard."

Troy smirked. "Keep your eye on the prize. If you do that, maybe there won't be any casualties, physical or emotional."

"Then what? You storm in and I get shot in the face once they realize I've turned them in?"

"We pull you out before they get a chance."

Luke smiled. "You're so worried about my plan within the crew but yours is pretty lackluster too."

"Correct. There are no guarantees. But you knew that from the beginning."

"All this effort to get you what you need, and you can't even guarantee my safety? Doesn't seem fair."

Troy leaned in with dagger-eyes. "Fair? Who said anything about fair? Don't you get it? Your chosen life of crime has *guaranteed* that you're not and never will be a free man. You belong to us now. I suggest you cooperate."

****

Sophia's mind swirled with all the troubling things on her mind. She had problems that would drive anyone mad. But when Tony told her to get dressed for her date with Armando De Palma, she almost pulled out her gun and shot him herself.

Her hands spread out in disbelief. "What do you mean put on a nice dress?"

"Rocco wants you to go out with Armando and see what you think of him."

She wagged her pointer finger at him. "Not a chance."

"Oh, come on. Listen, I know the guy. He's a respectable member. I think it's a fine choice for you."

She stared at him with narrowed eyes until he finally broke.

"I get it. I get it. Armando is not Mr. Green Eyes but what are you going to do exactly? Rocco chose Armando, not Luke. You can fight him on this, but I don't think he's going to budge."

She pointed to her chest. "This is my life, Tony. Not his."

"Look, humor him. Just show up with that red lipstick and high heels and have a nice dinner. Have some pasta, drink some wine. You don't have to make out with the guy."

She shot him a death stare.

"At least go through with it. Maybe when Luke starts moving up in the ranks, you can start dropping hints about how much you like his right hook."

She breathed in, shutting her eyes. "I'm supposed to be in hiding. Doesn't make much sense if I'm out in public all the time going on dates."

"True, but Rocco insisted on this date. He must really think Armando is a great guy to risk your life."

"Or he couldn't care less about my life and it's more about keeping up with appearances."

"Oh, come on. That's not true. Rocco loves you and you know it. He made you the boss, didn't he?"

"Is that love, Tony? Or is that strategy?"

"Listen, I'm not getting in between family matters. At the end of the day, I'm doing my job whether I like it or not because I took an oath."

Sophia rolled her eyes. The oath was beginning to mean less and less to her by the minute.

"If it makes you feel better, I'm going to be there anyway with Loverboy," Tony said, winking at her. "We're having a dinner meeting to discuss his next boxing match. Sammy couldn't make it tonight since Francesca's been feeling ill."

She waved her arms. "Oh, great. Even better. And what's Luke going to think about all this?"

Tony shrugged. "Honestly, he doesn't get to have an opinion. I like the guy but this is business."

She nodded. "Exactly right, Tony. That's the problem with this, it's not business, it's the rest of my life."

"All right, listen. No one's making you marry the guy. I'm pretty sure he hasn't picked out the ring yet." He tapped the face of his watch. "Let's get going, you're going to be late."

"Fine." She walked up the stairs to her bedroom and slammed the door shut. It wasn't fine. It was awful. Now she had to get dressed up to go on a date with someone she wasn't interested in, while Luke watched them from a distance in the same restaurant. All because of Rocco's old-school ways.

Nope, it wasn't going to be fine.

****

An hour later, Sophia came back down the stairs wearing the oldest and most ill-fitting frock she could find in her closet—which was not an easy task given her love for buying expensive clothes. She knew she looked the worst with her hair tied up and slicked back and her exaggerated black kohl-rimmed eyes resembled those of a raccoon. She looked terrible and that's exactly how she wanted to look.

Tony stared at her up and down. "That's a choice. You look comfortable and edgy at the same time."

"Exactly. That's what I'm going for. What's wrong with a woman wanting to be cozy?"

"Nothing." He lifted his elbow out for her to hold. "I'm pretty sure that's Armando's type."

"What a coincidence."

"Indeed, you two were made for each other."

She smacked his shoulder with her clutch. "Let's get this over with."

"Yes, Boss."

****

As soon as she opened the door to Isabella's, a wave of deafening chatter stopped Sophia in her tracks. "Wow, busy tonight. Surely, my hitman is here slurping spaghetti noodles with a delicious marinara."

Tony winked in her direction. "Or maybe it's vodka sauce."

She didn't respond to his alluding to Carmine's love of vodka sauce. But she did sense someone watching her enter the restaurant. A quick scan and her eyes met Luke staring in her direction with a furrowed brow.

Ugh.

Her stomach sank. Not only was she not in hiding but she was about to have dinner with some guy while Luke watched eagle-eyed from his table. She avoided his gaze and followed Tony toward a small table in the corner. Standing there, tall and burly, was her date, Armando.

Smiling with flushed chubby cheeks, he wiped his forehead with a handkerchief and placed it back into his blazer top pocket. At least he hadn't wiped his sweat with his hand.

"Armando, this is Sophia," Tony said, introducing them.

"Your beauty supersedes everything I've heard about you," Armando said.

"Thank you," she replied with a tight mouth.

"Shall we?" he asked, pulling one of the seats out for her—the one facing Luke.

"Right," Sophia replied, placing her clutch on the table and letting him push her seat in.

"I'll let you two get to know each other," Tony said, turning toward Sophia. "My table is not too far if you need anything."

"I hope your pasta is mushy," she said under her breath.

He smirked and went to his table.

"When Rocco reached out to me, I was truly honored he thought so highly of me to go out with you," Armando said, eyes locked on her.

"Rocco isn't thinking of anyone else. Trust me."

His smile faded.

Gio, the maître d', came around to their table.

"Sophia, good to see you. We have an amazing menu for you two tonight." He made a chef's kiss gesture, then placed two glasses of champagne on the table. "The wine pairing will complement each dish, and we will start with champagne."

"Thank you, Gio," Sophia said as he walked away. She watched Armando as he ripped apart a piece of bread and slathered it with butter, picturing herself in this scenario with him over and over again while everyone they knew would mysteriously disappear one by one— her worst nightmare.

Her eyes slid over to Luke's table. She'd seen that expression before, the one intent on jumping over the table and strangling his opponent. Squirming in her seat while Luke looked on, she took a large gulp of champagne. "Do you go on many dates?"

He swallowed his third piece of bread. "I've been on a few dates, but meeting women is hard enough considering my line of work. I went out with Antonia Castanzo about a month ago, but she never called me back."

"I know her. She's always had her eye on Mickey Bernardi, but he never seemed that interested in her."

From the corner of her eye, Sophia could see Luke's arms flailing in what appeared to be a heated conversation with Tony. She wondered if they were arguing about how many boxing matches Sammy wanted him to be in over the next few weeks. But Luke's eyes kept finding hers, making her think he wasn't happy about Tony's romantic setup.

"Mickey's a prick," Armando declared. "She can have him for all I care."

Sophia smiled. "You can do better." She couldn't

help feeling bad for him. Rocco made him go on this date regardless of how he might actually feel about her. Although Armando would rise in status if he somehow managed to pull this off, she could never go through with it, even if her life depended on it. "In fact, I might know someone more suitable for you. Her name is Alessandra Bianchi. She is quite the sweetheart and quite beautiful."

He smiled sheepishly. "I appreciate that, but Rocco might not be all right with that plan."

Her eyes caught Luke standing up. She wondered if he was planning on storming out or worse.

She turned her eyes back to Armando. "Don't you worry about Rocco. I'll deal with him."

Before Gio could bring them the menus, Luke marched over to their table, leaving Tony behind.

Sophia stared at her plate not wanting to make eye contact with anyone; the rhythmic sound of her heart pounded in her ears. A fight inside Isabella's would not go over well with the rest of the crew. She hoped Luke would not behave as the others might in this scenario.

He stopped, standing next to Armando's chair. His eyes fixed on Sophia, he placed his hand on Armando's right shoulder. "I don't blame you for going on this date with Sophia—anyone with half a brain would." His voice came out calm but firm. "But I am quite sure she is not here of her own free will."

Armando peered up at Luke. "She's free to come and go as she pleases."

"I'm also quite sure that you understand this situation is more complex and neither of you are acting of your own free will."

Armando cleared his throat and shook his head, seemingly irritated by Luke's assumptions.

"In the interest of being honest with ourselves, I propose you decide there is not enough interest in this relationship and someone else has caught your eye."

"And what if I don't?"

Luke smiled and squeezed his shoulder. "We'll figure it out over at Frank's Gym. It's your choice." He removed his hand from Armando's shoulder and walked toward the exit without making eye contact with Sophia.

Ordinarily, this kind of threat might create an all-out war within the crew. But most of the members didn't want to fight within the ranks or create a problem with the boss. She knew Armando wasn't up for this kind of threat and was unlikely to say anything to Rocco or push this any further than was necessary. She also noted that Luke's behavior tonight resembled that of other members of the mafia—an observation she didn't particularly like.

Sophia drank down the rest of her champagne. "So, about Alessandra."

Chapter Seventeen

Luke watched Kid's knee bounce as they sat a few feet away from each other in the back office of Luigi's pizza joint. They'd been told to meet in the office and wait for further instructions. He hoped Sammy hadn't set up another fight, unless this time it was with Kid. Truth is, he would have no problem smashing his fist into Kid's face with his good hand if there were any chance he'd been the one orchestrating the hits on Sophia.

Once Sammy finally arrived, he stood in front of them as if they were his students in class. "Since the Boss is in hiding, I've been sent to give the good news. This is where Luke will be connecting with his street team contacts, setting up the online business and Kid will be his assistant."

As soon as the words came out of Sammy's mouth, Kid yelped. "Oh, come on! His assistant? Don't I have a say in this?"

"No, as the newest member, you don't."

Kid slapped his knee. "What's the point of this?"

"You need a good mentor. We're under pressure to make sure Sophia is protected. Tony and I don't have time to micromanage new recruits. Luke will be setting up his contacts and you'll help him with day-to-day operations. You'll learn the business side and then hopefully branch out on your own. Plus, you can get free pizza downstairs any time you want. Sounds like a great setup to me. *Capisce*?"

Kid sat back in his chair and nodded without making eye contact.

"Good. I don't want to hear about any problems between you two. Remember, we're all on the same team."

"So, you'd think," Luke said, glancing at Kid. The thought of having to tolerate this jerk-off twerp for who knows how long made him want to pull out of this and do his prison time.

"We're all in agreement?" Sammy looked at them with his arms out. "Wonderful." He clapped his hands together. "I'll leave you to it and will be checking in to see the progress. I've got to check on Francesca. The hospital said she could go home today."

"Tell her I said get well," Luke said. "Your wife is a lovely person."

"Agreed," Kid repeated.

"Thanks, I will. Anyway, talk soon." Sammy took each step down the stairs with care.

Luke imagined it was hard to coordinate each step with one eye.

"You heard the man. Start learning stuff," Luke said.

"Learn what? How to be a jerk?"

Luke chuckled. "You've got that down solid. Maybe you could be a little nicer from now on."

Kid leaned forward, looking around to make sure no one else was around. "Hey, I know a guy from the Esposito family. His name is Enzo. He reached out to me to see if I was interested in a side hustle for a little bit of cash."

Luke stared at him. "I'm sorry? You're talking to the Esposito family, known enemy to the Costa Crew? Have you lost your mind?"

Kid shrugged. "Business is business and don't tell me a little more cash doesn't tempt you. Enzo said he's got some slot machines he leases to some of the casinos on the strip. He says they rack in a ton of cash."

"Why do you need him? Why don't you go on your own?"

"He owns all the machines. I don't have that kind of cash. He needs some brawn to rough up guys that don't pay."

Luke lifted a brow. "And you're the *brawn*?" He pointed at Kid. "No, you are."

Luke's blood boiled. "You offered me up to a rival crew member?"

"Rules, rules. I'm talking about cold hard cash here, not some childish beef between groups. No one in his crew has the guts, so he came to me."

"Of course he did. You're known for this type of shenanigans. Why do you think it took you so long to become a member? You realize if anyone heard this, you'd be toast."

Kid pursed his lips. "Come on. Aren't you even tempted?"

The hairs on the back of Luke's neck stood up. Kid might be trying to set him up. If he went through with this scheme, Kid could go back and tell the guys and Luke would be dead before he could explain himself. Then in his vindication, Kid would say he was right about Luke all along in an effort to become the favorite.

"Hell, no! You're insane. I want no part of this." Luke stood up, and in a need to cool off, walked away.

"Oh. Come on," Kid said. "Relax."

Luke raked a hand through his hair, took a couple

deep breaths, then went back over to Kid. "And what makes you think I won't tell the guys what you're up to? You'd be cast off and buried in cement at the bottom of a lake. I could blackmail *you*."

Kid stared back with his lips pressed into a hard line. "I never said I was actually involved with them. They approached me and I thought you might be interested. It might help ease up on the rivalry too." He pointed to his chest. "I'm looking out for our crew and the needs of the organization."

"Yeah, sure you are."

"Anyway, you'd never tell the guys." He waved his hand dismissively. "You don't have it in you."

Luke's stomach twisted as he turned away. Kid was right. He didn't have it in him. He wasn't the hero mobster boxing champ he'd been impersonating for months. He wasn't the bad guy.

"If you change your mind, you know where to find me," Kid said, reclining into the brown leather chair. "I'm going to take a nap—too many shots last night."

"You do that," Luke replied, watching him fall asleep within seconds of closing his eyes. He walked over to his desk, sinking into his seat, defeated by the constant dodging of bullets, even from his own crew. Staying on his toes until the end would be the only way to survive—however long that would be.

As he turned, he noticed an envelope labeled with his name laying on top of the desk. He stared at the writing, a distinct feminine cursive, knowing the moment he opened it marked the beginning of the end of everything. As he tapped the envelope on the desk, his breath quickened, and he shifted several times in his seat, hesitating to open it.

His mind swirled with the cascade of consequences his next set of steps would create. His relationship with Sophia would be over. Tony and Sammy would hate him and wish him dead despite how well they've been getting along. Then the Feds would take him somewhere completely foreign to live out the rest of his pathetic life and try to move on from all the pain he'd caused everyone. And *when* would it begin? How would the Feds decide the right moment? How long did he have?

Rubbing his eyes in exhaustion, he proceeded to open the envelope. Inside Sophia had written out account numbers and contacts to begin setting up his business on the laptop provided and instructions on how to launder the money through the pizza place.

This was it, the beginning of the end.

His mind went to the hard plastic device wedged in his shoe, knowing it was taping everything being said. He unlocked his phone and clicked on one of his contacts. "Hey, Vinny. How are you? Good. Good. I know it's been a while but I'm going to need your help with something huge. That's right, I'm back in business."

Chapter Eighteen

After three weeks of hiding out in her house in virtual solitude, Sophia decided to go against her crew's advice and checked herself into Cliff's Inn. It was a motel fourteen miles from her place and she could lounge in the sun and let her skin turn golden without anyone knowing.

Tony, of course, realized she had disappeared within a few hours and incessantly called her until she finally answered her phone. "What have you done?"

He yelled so loud she had to hold the phone away from her ear. "Nothing, I can't stay in the house all day and all night, Tony. Have a heart."

"Have a heart? If you get shot in the heart I can't help you. Where are you?"

"If I tell you, don't come looking for me. I need a couple days off."

Silence.

"I mean it, Tony. I need a break."

She heard him sighing through the phone. "Two days. If you don't come back, I'm sending the boys out with handcuffs and rope."

She snickered. "Fine. Two days. I'm at Cliff's Inn. But I'm warning you, don't come find me."

"Ugh, what a dump. I wouldn't want to come find you there anyway. What an embarrassment to the organization."

"That's the point, Tony. No one would expect to find me here. They'd expect you to book me a five-star hotel on the Las Vegas strip. But I don't need all that. I just want some space."

"Don't draw any attention to yourself and on principle I'm not going to tell you to enjoy it."

She smiled from ear to ear, enjoying his pretentious nature. "I'm good with that."

He hung up on her and she was fine with that—a welcome break from the mafia life. In fact, she couldn't believe how free she felt without the weight of an illegal organization on her back. But the sickening pang in her stomach was a constant reminder that she missed Luke. A lot. Once she'd left her house, she thought he'd be worried and come find her as he always had. He did not. She wondered if he'd finally pulled the plug on their relationship for good. Her heart ached at the thought that he could so easily walk away, deciding that their relationship would only be about business, and she would live out the rest of her days as someone else's loyal and dutiful wife.

Lifting her eyes from the novel she'd brought to escape reality but was too distracted by her intrusive thoughts to read, she noticed a stocky man with a shaved head reclined in one of the lounge chairs a few feet away from her. Dressed in black trousers, a white long-sleeve button-down shirt and black sunglasses, she thought it odd he was not wearing bathing suit trunks to lounge under the scorching sun. Odd and suspicious indeed.

As she shot up from the lounge chair, the beach towel sticking to her sweaty back, she realized they'd found her. Rapid beats struck her chest as it became clear the hitman she'd been trying so hard to hide from sat a few feet away from her.

Her mind went to the small pistol she carried with her at all times in her purse back in the room. She had recovered it in the crystal cave after Tony had shot down Duke. It would be risky, but she had to get to her room.

Grabbing her towel, phone, and sunglasses, she slid off the chair and hustled around the opposite side of the pool to get to the back door of the motel. She hoped he wouldn't shoot her in the back on her way inside. Holding her breath, she opened the back door and made it inside. Not wasting another second, she bolted to her room at the end of the hall.

Her flip-flops slapped against her feet as she ran, almost tripping over them. Fumbling with her room key, she slid it in and turned. Taking a second to glance down the hall before entering her room, relief flooded her body as no one had gone through the back door as of yet. She pushed the door open and slammed it shut behind her, locking every latch and chain.

Catching her breath, she wasted no time changing out of her black two-piece bathing suit. After she was back in her black pencil skirt, white blouse, and stilettos, she pulled the gun out of her purse and sat at the edge of the bed, waiting. The silence in her ears was louder than a gunshot going off nearby. She breathed out slowly to calm her racing pulse. A small snicker escaped her lips. The idea that the hitman was lounging next to her in the sun, fully dressed and in plain sight, now sounded ludicrous. Maybe the poor guy forgot to pack his swim trunks, and she had severely overreacted—wouldn't be the first time.

A few seconds later, she heard the unmistakable sound of someone running down the hall. She gripped the gun tighter, praying it was just a teenager with too much energy until, *bam!* Heart in her throat, she pointed her gun at the door ready to shoot if the hitman made it through. But another crash against her door didn't come. Instead, she heard muffled grunting sounds. Placing her ear against the door, she could hear cursing and groaning as she realized there was a struggle going on outside her door. She thought maybe someone had called the cops on the suspicious man by the pool. But opening the door would only seal her fate. She'd let the cops deal with him and then she would return home where her crew would be around to protect her—that is, after they lectured her on making better decisions for the future.

Bang!

She jolted at the unmistakable sound of a gun going off, followed by a deep groan. Then silence. Panicking, she weighed her options of opening the door now to something grisly and potentially dangerous or barricading herself in the room until somebody else dealt with it.

"Sophia?" An unknown man called to her from the other side of the door. Then he knocked. "You're safe now. You can open the door. He's gone."

Something about the voice seemed non-threatening enough but could she trust it?

"Who are you?" she said through the door.

"My name is Vinny. I'm a friend of Luke Daniels."

Her throat seized up, making it difficult to speak. "He sent you?"

"He did. He said someone might be looking for you, and sure enough, he was right. I caught him slipping through the back door not long after you left the pool area. He certainly looked suspicious in his black suit and fedora—creepy old man with a wrinkled face."

Sophia's heart stopped. Carmine? "Is he dead?"

"I'm pretty certain he is dead."

Since she'd previously heard Luke talk about this Vinny person as his current business partner and friend, she felt confident about opening the door a small crack. The man she'd been talking to on the opposite side of the door was the same one she'd seen reclining next to by the pool.

"I need to start working on getting rid of the body," he said in a matter-of-fact tone.

He behaved professionally but she detected a kindness in his large brown eyes.

She nodded, and her eyes went toward the ground. Lying crumbled on the dark blue carpet was Carmine Bruno with no signs of life. Relief and disgust swept through her body. To think this man had caused so much fear in her life and now it was over. Before she snapped the door shut to let her bodyguard get to work on cleanup, the glint of a gold medallion around Carmine's neck caught her eye. The round pendant lay face-up on the carpet. She leaned in closer to inspect the piece.

The gold piece featured the head of a lion with a tiny diamond inside its mouth, something she instantly recognized as belonging to her late father. He'd worn the necklace day in and day out for as long as she could remember until the day he never returned home again. The only way it would have come off his neck is if someone had taken it from his cold body and that person had apparently been Carmine.

"You can take the chain if you want as a souvenir. People do it all the time."

"It was my father's. How brazen Carmine was to

wear it around me. I was so caught up in my own issues I hadn't even noticed."

"He stole it from your father?"

She nodded, reaching down to find the clasp and release the chain from his neck. She squeezed the medallion in her hand, never wanting to lose sight of it. "I think this confirms who was behind my father's murder."

Vinny breathed in deeply. "I'm sorry you had to go through this, but I am glad you're getting some closure."

"Thank you for helping me out. I'll pack up my things and head out shortly."

"No problem. If there's anything else I can do for you let me know how I can assist. Luke's a good friend and I owe him a favor."

Of course he did. In one way or another, Luke was probably the hero to everyone he'd encountered in his life. "It looks like you're even now. Thanks again," she said, closing the door.

In a sudden rush to get back to the life she wanted to escape, she began throwing her clothes and shoes in her carry-on any way they would fit. She hadn't planned on being away that long and the idea of returning home should've been a comforting thought but now it filled her with dread. Carmine was dead and his crew would be looking for an explanation. The organization as she knew it would no longer be the same.

The Costa Crew was in trouble, and it was all her fault.

****

A storm of emotions assaulted Luke's mind as he struggled to come to grips with the fallout of his actions. Sophia knelt on her knees in front of her father's gravestone, Anthony Costa. Her mother, Serafina, stood over her wearing a black dress and matching lace veil covering her jet-black hair. He and the other crew members had decided to meet in the graveyard following the death of Carmine Bruno. He watched as she leaned to place a bouquet of lilies by the headstone and then reached around her neck to clasp a gold necklace she'd pulled out of her leather jacket. Holding up the medallion to her lips, she gave it a kiss.

Her mother began to cry, pushing a handkerchief to her falling tears. Then Sophia stood and the pair walked over to join the rest of her crew.

"Barbarian," Serafina said to the group with venom in her voice. "Can you believe he took Anthony's favorite chain? He never took it off."

"And now his daughter will wear it," Luke said.

"I'll never take it off," Sophia said.

The sadness in her eyes tugged at his heart.

"How's your wrist, Ms. Costa?" Luke asked, noticing her cast.

"Doctor said I broke it in two places," Serafina said, staring up at him, her eye color more of a gray-blue hue. "I probably need surgery. I'm not looking forward to that. I hate hospitals."

He noted Sophia must've inherited her legendary eye color from her father. "I'll come with you to the hospital if you want," Luke said.

Serafina reached out, grabbing his jaw, her long red nails digging into his skin. "You're such a good boy. You and Sophia should go on a date." She gently tapped his cheek, smiling wide with a bit of red lipstick on her teeth. "You two would look so good together."

Luke's eyes caught Sophia's before they both

bowed their heads in embarrassment.

Tony cleared his throat.

"Mom, don't say that," Sophia said.

"What? I'm telling the truth. That's what I think."

"With sincerest apologies, Ms. Costa," Sammy interjected, "now is not the time for distractions for them. There is a lot going on right now—"

"All right, Sammy. I understand. It's about business," Serafina said. "Why don't you all come to my house for something to eat? I have a pot of sauce on the stove that simmered all morning and some fresh bread from the bakery."

"That sounds amazing," Tony said, never one to turn down a delicious meal.

"I think we have to pass," Sammy said. "There's a lot we need to discuss first."

"All right, I understand. I'm not worried at all. I know you'll figure it out. Carmine had a lot of enemies and he needed to go. Good riddance."

"I wish it were that simple," Sammy said.

"Me too," Sophia said.

Observing her disheartened expression, Luke knew for Sophia, discovering that Carmine had indeed been the hitman and her father's murderer had been a double-edged sword. On one hand, she would get the closure she needed and freedom she craved from Carmine's death but at a cost.

The rest of the crew, justifiably, had concern etched on their faces. He'd sent Vinny to protect Sophia, but he hadn't expected Carmine to show up. Had he known, he would've given explicit instructions to let him live. Now the future of the group was in jeopardy, and he'd disappointed its members. Sammy, Tony, and even Kid had become his buddies, whether he intended to do so or not, and their disheartened feelings weighed heavily on his mind.

"I'm sorry, guys. I thought I was doing the right thing," Luke said with downcast eyes.

Silence. No one wanted to speak first. Everyone's hesitation made him feel even worse. "But if I hadn't sent Vinny, she'd probably be dead. Who knew Carmine would follow her out there?"

"Fighter, we know you had Sophia's best interests in mind, and he deserved what he got for whacking her father and threatening her life." Sammy rubbed his eyes. "I just wish it hadn't been Carmine of all people."

Luke nodded in agreement.

"This is my fault," Sophia said, sniffing. "If I hadn't left the house, Luke wouldn't have felt the need to have me followed, but if Carmine hadn't followed me, I may have never known he had anything to do with my father."

"It's a tough situation. There's nothing we can do to reverse it," Sammy said. "What happened to Carmine probably would've happened eventually. I thought we could try and keep the peace for a while, but things sped up a bit." He turned to Tony. "And where were you?"

"She's a grown woman. I did my best." Tony raised his arms out in frustration.

"He's right," Sophia chimed in. "I'm not a robot. I was getting fed up with this place and wanted to get out for a few days. It was a bad decision. But I do agree that Carmine was always going to be a problem. It was just a matter of time, and this proved my point that he was deeply involved in trying to get rid of me. In fact, he was probably the ringleader behind all the attacks against me. He hated that Rocco had chosen me over him to become boss. Good riddance if you ask me too."

"Hear, hear," Tony said.

"That being said, we need a plan," Sammy said. "Carmine's crew is amassing bullets and sharpening knives as we speak."

"Can't they elect a new leader within their crew?" Luke asked.

"They can and they likely will do that soon, but Carmine's crew will want retribution," Sammy explained.

"What about money? What if they were paid off?"

"It might help and usually works for most people but there's an honor code the crews live by, and I wouldn't be surprised if they burst in and start shooting one of these days."

"Carmine was killed by someone they can't trace to us. How can they retaliate if a random person was involved?"

"He was killed in the same location where Sophia was staying. They'll probably assume her crew had something to do with Carmine's death. So, when they come looking for us, we should be ready."

Sophia chuckled.

"What's funny?" Luke asked as the entire crew looked at her like she was nuts.

"I've got good news and bad news. The bad news is we have a potentially violent internal war on our shoulders."

"I'm assuming it's the good news that's funny?" Sammy asked.

She shook her head. "None of it is funny but it just dawned on me that I'm free." She smiled. "Free from the hitman. It means I can go wherever I please whenever I please and right now I want to forget these problems and go to Lucky Guess for a drink." She winked in Luke's direction. "Care to join me, anyone?"

"I think it's well deserved," Tony said. "Let's all go."

Luke smiled with his head down. He was glad to give her that moment of freedom and closure regarding her father's death. Years of feeling trapped can make a person go mad. But his smile would be short-lived, knowing her freedom would be temporary for his own gain. As soon as Troy rang the bell, everyone around him would go to prison, trapped by concrete for the rest of their lives—certainly nothing to celebrate. The heaviness in his heart made him wonder if he could continue to play the role of the bad guy when his motives were infinitely worse. He realized, probably not.

Chapter Nineteen

"All I can say is, *wow*. You really outdid yourself," Troy said in between bites of food. His eyes remained on his plate as he struggled to cut through a tough piece of meat. "At first things were going very well when you captured details of their pizza joint money laundering operation." He chuckled and pointed the knife at Luke. "But boy, I was not prepared to hear about the murder of Carmine Bruno and who was behind it."

Luke shrugged. "What was I supposed to do? Let him kill her?"

Troy stopped chewing and stared with cold eyes. "Yes. Even better. Let them kill each other. Let the universe take its course. They're on the wrong side of the fence, remember?"

Luke dragged in a deep, ragged breath. The recent revelation that he could no longer remain Troy's puppet, out to destroy everyone's life to save his own, had come to him fast and unrelenting. He was no longer able to rationalize the dishonesty or tolerate the carnage he'd leave behind. Troy would have to fix this mess.

"I don't think I can do this anymore."

Troy put down his knife and stared at him. "Let's not make any rash decisions. What's the matter? What's changed?"

"It's gone too far."

"What's gone too far?"

"The deception. I can barely look at myself in the mirror anymore. I don't know who I am or who I am supposed to be."

"Let me help. You are Luke Daniels, convicted criminal and informant for the FBI." Troy studied his face. "What? Did you think you were *Fighter*? Boxer extraordinaire and member of the Costa Crew? That person doesn't exist. He's not real. You might *want* to be him but he's pure fiction, made up in order to get the criminals convicted and you off the hook."

Luke stared down at the table, unable to look Troy in the eyes. "I know that, but I can't do it anymore. Every day that passes makes me sicker and sicker to my stomach. I can't eat. I can't sleep. I want out."

"I don't think you mean that."

"I do mean it. I want out. I'm not cut out for this. At this point I can't tell who the bad guys are anymore."

Troy's lips formed into a thin hard line. "I see. This is unfortunate but I can't say your feelings surprise me. Sometimes when you're buried in the field with the enemy it can be confusing. I had a woman working for us as an informant in a counterintelligence case. She'd been a spy in the US for years." Troy chuckled. "Her rap sheet puts yours to shame. We sent her overseas using the skills she'd already acquired on her own. But after some time, she stopped reporting back to us. We thought her cover had been blown and she was gone forever. Turns out she fell in love with her captor. We never heard from her again."

"You're so good at telling horror stories."

"I'm not trying to change your mind, but I thought you would last a little longer."

"I did the best I could. I put myself in danger

multiple times. It's a surprise I haven't already been killed. I gave you what you needed." Luke leaned in. "At this point, the best option would be to cut me loose a little sooner than planned."

"Don't you want to think about this a little bit more?"

Luke shook his head. "Nope. I have nothing left to give."

Troy said nothing.

"There's one more thing."

"Oh, I didn't realize today was your day to make demands. Tell me, what else can I do for you?"

"I want Sophia to come with me."

Troy's nostrils flared. "We don't owe you or her anything. We gave you the opportunity to walk away free and clear from a major prison sentence in exchange for some information. Sounds like a good deal to me."

"At what price? I still have to start over in a strange place and watch people I care about go down because of me. I betrayed them and I'll have to live with that forever."

"That's right. You will live with that because they are mobsters, not you."

Luke shook his head. "Sometimes I'm just not so sure."

"Are you asking me to take her out with you? To ignore all the illegal business deals and murders she ordered and sanctioned as the boss of the Costa Crew? Are you asking me to go against the government?"

Luke said nothing, too embarrassed to admit he wanted exactly that. The line between good and bad had become so blurred he barely recognized himself. He was sure he'd become a different person, but who was he now? A pseudo-gangster? A boxer for hire?

"And what do you think will happen? Will you and Sophia be together in a new town? Will your relationship work outside of the Costa Crew? Does she even want the same thing you do?"

All very good questions. He shrugged. "I don't have all the answers, but I can only go by how I feel, and I am one hundred percent sure that I'm done with being your informant."

Troy leaned back in his booth seat. The confusion on his face signaled he was struggling with doing the right thing versus doing what he'd been trained to do all his life. "This goes against anything that I would do myself or would want for you but frankly, I'm sick of hearing about your identity crisis. I'd rather we deal with this issue here and now rather than hear about your ultimate demise down the road simply because I wouldn't listen."

"Smart man."

"The decision is yours. What do you want to do?"

Luke's stomach flipped as he realized his whole world was about to change. But in his heart, he knew what he wanted. "Pull me out."

****

"I owe you my life again," Sophia said with a snicker as she let Luke into her house. "How could you have known I was itching to come out of hiding and where I would end up?"

"You dropped some hints about wanting to get out of the house. I knew it was only a matter of time and when Tony told me you'd actually done it, I had Vinny track you down at the motel. He's super talented at finding people who don't want to be found."

"He seemed nice enough."

Luke shrugged. "I guess if you think being a ruthless killer is nice but then again, that is what you've been around most of your life."

"True." She examined his face. The corners of his mouth were downturned, his eyes vacant. Something seemed off. "What's wrong?"

"We need to talk." Instead of waiting for a response, he walked into her kitchen, grabbed a tumbler from her cabinet, filled it with bourbon and stared down at the black marble island.

His words stung. How many times had she heard that phrase and nothing good had come of it? The worst was when her mother had to tell her and Rocco that her father was never coming home again.

She followed reluctantly behind him. A minute ago she'd been more hopeful about her future as her situation had drastically improved. She'd been freed from the hitman and from a life in hiding. How quickly that feeling was eclipsed.

He took a drink, deep enough to drain half the glass. "I have something to tell you."

Ugh. She hated that line. Her jaw clenched.

"But first I want to know what you want. I need to know if you want to continue to be the mob boss of the Costa Crew."

She stared at the ground, shaking her head. "I never wanted to be the boss." Her arms went out. "Let's face it, I am barely the boss. Sammy and Tony have done a lot for me, but I've always wanted something different. I never wanted the role of the dutiful wife either, resigned to existing in the background and pretending I didn't know what was going on."

"I believe you, but I need to know that you're not using me to escape your life."

Her throat seized up. That hurt. "How can you say that when you're the one who has been pushing me away?"

"With good reason."

Another punch to the gut. "How so?"

He hesitated, draining the last bit of bourbon. "I've been lying to you."

Sophia's stomach sank. He'd come to break up with her again and like a fool she would likely try to stop him. "It can't be that bad."

"It is. I need to tell you everything."

Her knees trembled as she turned around and barely made it to the couch to sit. "Tell me." She couldn't bear to look at him but could feel him staring at her.

"I'm not who you think I am."

She met his gaze, worried now about her safety. Where had she placed her gun, and could she get to it in time?

"It doesn't change how I feel about you, but you will hate me for a while. I would rather tell you the truth and hope that maybe you'll find a reason to forgive me."

The lump in her throat made it hard to talk. "You're scaring me. What did you do?"

"I've been working for the Feds in exchange for no prison time for my past drug trafficking charges."

Searing pain spread throughout her skull. She couldn't believe what she was hearing. To break up with her because he didn't want to date the boss or found it awkward around the other guys was one thing, but not this. This was far worse. There was no coming back from this. Her mind raced through all the clues she'd missed.

Admittedly, she'd had reservations about an outsider coming out of nowhere and asking to be part of the Costa Crew, but she ignored those clues, wanting a change in her life so badly and becoming dazzled by his skills. And what did that mean for their relationship? Had he faked the whole thing?

"You're an informant? A snitch?"

"I'm sorry I let it go on this long, but I didn't know what to do."

She stood up, and angry tears ran down her cheeks. "You didn't know what to do? You betrayed all of our trust. Do you realize you're sending everyone to prison?"

"I didn't expect to care that Sammy liked his eggs runny with crispy bacon, swimming in hot sauce or that Tony chewed gum in his sleep to keep his breath fresh. In the beginning, all I cared about was doing whatever the Feds needed me to do to stay out of prison, but then I found myself caring a lot about the crew to the point where I could no longer keep up with the charade. And I didn't expect to fall in love with you either."

Something other than the muscles in her body held her upright in the moment. Perhaps it was the fragment of hope she'd been holding onto that he'd reciprocate what she'd been feeling since the day she laid eyes on him inside Lucky Guess. A shocked but delighted gasp escaped her lips.

"Come with me."

Her eyes went wide. "Come with you? What does that mean? Where would we go?"

"I think I can get the Feds to let you join me in witness protection. You can start over with a new life. You won't have to answer to your brother or continue to live in the organization. It's what you've wanted."

She paused at the enormity of what he was proposing. He'd deceived her from the day they'd met. Any rational person would think going with him was insanity. At least in her current situation, she had people who loved her or at least protected her. Walking away meant giving all of that up. "What about the guys? They'll all go to prison for the rest of their lives while I get to go free?" More tears streamed down her face as he approached her, grabbing her hands, squeezing them gently.

"There is no other way. Your life belonged to the organization. Eventually, you and the guys would either be going to prison, or you would end up dead. I can't save the guys, but I can save you."

She stared at the ground. Her whole life flashed before her eyes. Nothing would ever be the same and she didn't know whether that was good or bad. Without much hesitation, the words slipped out of her mouth as if she'd known her decision all along. "How long do I have?"

"Not long. I think the Feds will strike in a day or so but of course they won't tell me exactly when."

"Where will they take us?"

"I don't know. It could be anywhere."

As she calmed herself down, she tried to imagine a different life—possibly a normal one with Luke somewhere she'd never been before. No one would know her past or know what she'd done or been through. It would be a fresh start. "Can I think about it?"

He frowned at her. "What do you need to think about? I know it's a lot to process but we don't have much time. The wheels are already in motion. Don't you want to go with me?"

She nodded. "I do, very much."

He came closer, pulling her chin up toward him. His sage green eyes were bright and hopeful. "You can trust me. This is a good thing. I promise." He kissed her lips in assurance and let go of her hands. "I'll come see you tomorrow and keep you posted if I know more about the Feds' plans. You can't tell anyone, not even Tony."

"I know," she said, tearing up again. "I won't."

"It will feel like death at first but then you will have a real life."

She nodded, trying to force a slight smile.

"All right, see you soon." He slowly walked toward the door but then stopped and turned around. "And Sophia."

Her stomach flipped. She couldn't take it if there was more. "Yes?"

"Don't run."

Chapter Twenty

Sweat beads dotted Luke's forehead as he watched Kid throw sharpened pencils at a makeshift paper target he'd pinned to the wall. Any minute. The Feds would burst in wearing full assault gear, slamming Kid on the ground while holding huge guns to his face. Troy's scheme would be over, and the people Luke had been calling his friends for the last few months would all go to jail. The train had left the station full speed ahead and there was nothing he could do to stop it. If he attempted to block the arrest he'd be shot point blank. He couldn't save them from the Feds. His sole comfort was that maybe Sophia had seen it his way. Maybe she would give up the life she didn't want and make a change that included him in her life. Maybe she hadn't run.

Bam! Luke jumped in his seat as the entrance door to the office slammed open.

"Hey, I didn't mean to scare you," Sammy said, carrying a large pizza pie box as he stormed into the office. "I brought pizza."

Luke let out his breath, covering his face with his hands.

"What's the matter, Fighter?" Tony said, coming in behind Sammy. "You seem a little jumpy. Don't you like pizza?"

"What's this, a party?" Luke asked. "Should we be all hanging out here like this together?"

"Ah, come on," Sammy said. "We're just having pizza." He placed the box on the table and pointed at Luke. "Why? Who's listening? Are you wearing a wire?"

Luke swallowed hard. "No, why would you think that?"

Sammy laughed. "Come on, Fighter, live a little." He grabbed a huge dripping cheese slice. "Here, have some pizza. You seem a little tense."

"FBI! Get down!" A man's voice yelled from the doorway.

Luke stood up and then fell backward onto his chair. Rolling onto his stomach, he crawled away from the entrance. From his spot on the floor, he saw six agents in the office with guns pointed at Sammy, Kid, and Tony. None of the crew had obeyed the command to get on the floor.

"Get on the ground now!" the agents shouted in unison.

Kid, Sammy, and Tony all looked in Luke's direction. They knew. Kid clenched his jaw and went down to the ground. Sammy mouthed expletives in Luke's direction as he reluctantly obeyed. Tony didn't budge. Luke's heart ached as he watched the disappointment form in Tony's eyes. They'd become close. One could say they had developed a mutual respect for one another but all of that meant nothing in the face of betrayal.

Seemingly undeterred by the threat to his life, Tony remained standing. "You pigs, coming in here thinking you own the place. You don't have it in you."

"Tony," Sammy warned. "Get your butt on the ground now. We'll figure it out later."

"I don't want to figure it out later," Tony said, anger making his face red. "Who do they think they are coming into our place of business?"

"They're going to shoot you," Sammy continued with a stern tone.

"I don't think they will. In fact, I want to figure it out now." Tony reached into his jacket.

Luke shook his head, reaching his right arm out. "Tony, no!"

Shots rang out from all sides except from one agent who shouted, "Hold your fire!"

Luke tucked his head down, covering it with his hands. As fast as the shots were fired, they ended. He heard nothing but ringing in his ears. Strong arms pulled him off the floor. The same arms dragged him quickly toward the exit. But before Luke was taken from the scene, he glanced at the carnage. Anguish filled his body as he saw Tony's lifeless body.

Anger boiled to the surface as he struggled against his captor. "Let go of me. How could you do this?"

The vise grip on his arms loosened. The agent who'd picked him off the floor backed away and pulled off his hooded mask. "You knew this day would come. We're pulling you out. Let's go," Troy Wilson said, grabbing Luke's arms again.

Luke yanked free of his grip. "Why did you have to shoot him?"

"I didn't shoot him. He was reaching for a gun. My agents have every right to defuse the threat. That's what they're trained to manage."

Luke glared at him, unable to process what he'd just witnessed.

"It's not safe here. I don't want them to have the

opportunity to retaliate. We have to go now. Don't make me arrest you too," Troy barked.

As Luke headed down the stairs to the ground floor, Troy followed behind. "Look, I'm sorry but there's no guarantee that everyone gets out alive. Even for you."

Luke stopped at the bottom of the stairs. Only anger kept him from breaking down completely. "I know that. Do you know how many times you've told me?" He barreled through the doors where red lights flashed from dozens of law enforcement vehicles waiting outside to collect what they came for.

Troy pulled at Luke's arm. "Officially, you have to come with me. There's no getting around it."

Luke turned to face him. "Where am I going?"

"I can't tell you but it's going to be a long car ride and we need to leave now—"

A loud bang came from the door smashing open as Sammy and Kid were led handcuffed by agents toward the paddy wagon. Each one taking a glance at Luke, clearly plotting his death in their minds.

His stomach roiled as images of Tony's mangled body flooded his mind. "This doesn't feel right."

"Listen, you won. You're free. No prison time. You're still alive. You get to start over."

But Luke couldn't and wouldn't celebrate. He'd lost a friend. Tony was a good guy despite what he did for a living. Confusion racked his mind as he realized that while working as an informant, he'd been working for the bad guys all along.

"Let's go," Troy said, pressing on Luke's back. "You don't really have a choice. You run, we'll find you. This is your only option."

Luke reluctantly walked toward the car Troy would

be driving him into his new life. "What about Sophia?" His heart ached knowing how devastated she would be about Tony. She may never forgive him.

Troy stopped in front of the driver's side of the black sedan. "She ratted out Frankie Esposito and gave us some of the best information we've gotten so far in exchange for her freedom. She'll also be relocated far from here. You're both very lucky given the circumstances."

"Frankie Esposito?" Luke managed a slight smirk. "She ratted out the Costa Crew's main rival? That was smart. Even at the end, she was thinking about her crew."

"I doubt her crew will see it that way given her recent choices."

"Tony would've." Luke's chest ached at the sound of Tony's name, knowing he'd never see his bright white smile again or witness his complete devotion to protecting Sophia at all costs.

"Look, I'm sorry about the guy." Troy said. "These things happen. At some point you'll understand how lucky you are and maybe even thank me for going way past normal protocol to get Sophia out of there."

Luke shook his head. "I don't feel lucky."

"You took a gamble, and it paid off. Maybe you should look into playing card games."

Luke didn't answer.

"In any case, I'm sure you'll eventually understand that all of this happened for a reason that ultimately benefited you. Maybe you don't see it now, but you will and since you're unable to thank me now, I'll just say it for you, you're welcome."

****

Sophia stared at the snow-capped mountains outside

her kitchen window as she buttoned up her black cardigan—quite a change from the melting sun in Nevada. She had a new name and a new address designed to protect her from mafia retaliation. And would it? From what she knew about snitches, their time on earth was limited but she had chosen to live that short time on her terms rather than under someone else's rules. Even if no one came after her out here in the sticks, the guilt of ratting out her family and friends would probably consume her until there was nothing left. The only light in her life was Luke.

Devastation racked her body since the day she told her mother she'd chosen to go with Luke into witness protection. On that day, her mom wept into Sophia's shoulder so deeply, her sleeve had become sodden with tears.

"You're going off with that boy and leaving me here?"

"I want a different life, Mom. You've known that. I've said that to you forever."

"Rocco's in jail. You're leaving me forever. How can I go on like this?"

"I'll be happier. You can go on knowing that I will be better off with Luke."

"They'll find you and kill you for being a snitch, Sophia."

"I'm willing to take that chance. I'd rather live a life I chose than live like a zombie and a puppet. I promise we'll see each other again. Once I learn where we're going, I'll break the rules and tell you where we're living so you can come visit us."

Serafina smiled through the tears. "You promise?"

"I promise. This is not the last time we will see each

other, and who knows, maybe you'll have grandchildren to visit someday."

Even though her mom had instantly lit up to the possibility of Sophia having children, the meeting she'd had with her almost deterred her from leaving. In the end, she knew her mother would want her to be happy.

The Feds had provided them with a secluded bungalow forty minutes in all directions from any other signs of life. A few days had passed since she'd arrived at the bungalow. The quiet remoteness had been quite the shock to her system. Some days, the only sounds she heard all day were the drips of water landing in a puddle underneath the razor-sharp icicles forming on the roof's edge. She no longer wore her signature red lipstick and her black hair had been dyed blonde as she waited for Luke to arrive.

On the day she'd been picked up for relocation from her home in Nevada, someone had randomly knocked on her door. After Luke had divulged the truth to her about being an informant, she'd known that day was coming but couldn't be sure if someone from Carmine's crew had come to whack her either.

With her finger on the trigger of her gun, trembling but ready to fire, she'd opened her front door a small crack.

"Sophia Costa?" A woman's voice came from the other side of the door. "I'm Special Agent Dana Foster. It's time to go."

Sophia had thrown her luggage in the back of the gray sedan, which she'd packed ahead of time in preparation and got into the front seat. She'd studied Dana's brown shoulder-length hair, the tiny wing eyeliner at the edge of her hazel eyes and a whisper of pink lipstick on her lips. She hadn't expected a female agent.

"How long is the drive?" Sophia asked.

"Long," Dana said, keeping her eyes on the road.

"Do you know when Luke will get relocated?" Sophia asked, watching the desert landscape as they sped past in the early light.

"No."

Sophia turned her eyes toward Agent Foster, scanning the side of her face. Her mouth had closed into a hard line, her eyes concentrating hard on the road ahead. Sophia guessed they were about the same age, both with emotional hard edges from living strenuous lives but individually existing on different sides of the law. She felt a strange connection to her.

"I've done things I'm not proud of—horrible things," Sophia said, watching for a reaction. "But I don't regret any of it."

Nothing.

She continued. "I bet, in your line of work, you're used to shooting people from a distance, but nothing beats the gurgling sound when you slit someone's throat."

Dana put her right hand to her mouth, stifling a yawn as she continued to watch the road.

Sophia breathed in, contemplating how she might break through her facade during their long journey. "I wonder if you can imagine what it's like growing up in a household where everything is a secret and each day that passed you wondered if someone had decided on that particular day you were going to die."

No change from Dana.

Sophia continued to stare at the side of Dana's face.

"My father was killed by one of his own crew members when I was eleven years old."

Dana cleared her throat. "My brother died in the field during an overseas operation. He was also with the FBI. We were twins."

A breakthrough. "I'm so sorry for your loss. I'm sure he's happy to see you carry on with the missions."

"I bet your father is as well."

Sophia smiled, grabbing her medallion and giving it a squeeze. She had initially followed in his footsteps but now she wondered how her dad would really feel about her decision to leave the organization. Given he'd been murdered and left his young kids behind, she wanted to believe he would agree with her actions.

"Is it hard?" Sophia asked.

"Is what hard?"

"Always having to be tough?"

"You tell me."

She appreciated the empathy. "I think it made me a stronger person overall. How about you?"

Dana's mouth returned to a hard line. "I think it makes your life seem more tragic. We like to think tragedy makes us stronger people to help us cope but I don't believe you really move on from it."

"That's a hard pill to swallow."

"As it should be. Hopefully you have someone in your life who makes your tragedy more tolerable day in and day out."

Sophia looked out her window, the sunrise coating the mountains in a red-orange color. That someone was Luke. She'd known it from the minute she'd laid eyes on him. He saved her from her tragedy. "I do have someone."

Dana smiled. "Good. Cherish that person." Her smile faded as if remembering she had a job to do. "We need to talk about your transformation."

"Transformation into what?"

"Into someone else. You'll have a new identity, so we need a new look to match."

Sophia had never deviated from her usual look. She always had shiny long black hair, red lips and nails. It was her signature and everyone around her recognized her for it. A new look never occurred to her.

"I think you could be a blonde."

"Blonde?"

"With those eyes, I think you could even go platinum."

Sophia scrunched up her face.

Dana took a quick look and chuckled. "Don't worry. I'll help you."

Chapter Twenty-One

Luke stepped out of Troy's car into the chilly air dressed in the same short-sleeve shirt and trousers he had on when he left Nevada. Plucked out of thin air, he had brought nothing with him—not even a toothbrush.

He stared at the secluded bungalow tucked behind massive evergreen trees. The stony facade had a sharply curved roof and newly varnished window shutters. A set of irregular stone steps led up to the dark wooden door. The light coming from inside meant he'd finally get to see Sophia—a bittersweet feeling as he wondered how he was going to tell her about Tony.

Troy opened the trunk and chucked a duffel bag at him. "There are a few items in there to get you started— a new identity card and some cash. There's a computer inside the house for when you decide to look for work. I suggest something more on the legal side of things."

Luke stared at the snow-covered ground, feeling the cold breeze whip around his bare neck—a coat would've been helpful. "I want to sound grateful but I'm not so sure."

Troy breathed in. "Understandable. For whatever it's worth, I'll continue to apologize about Tony. It's been a long road to get here. You worked hard against all odds and won. Even if submerging yourself in their world has cost you something, there's at least a light at the end of the tunnel." He gestured toward the bungalow.

Sophia. He would be living with the former mob boss of the Costa Crew—two dangerous criminals living in the middle of nowhere. Luke smiled at the absurdity of it all. He hadn't smiled in a while. "For that I will thank you," he said, finally looking Troy in the eyes.

Troy nodded and entered his car. "I'll check in on you here and there," he said, his head leaning out of the window. "It's been a pleasure working with you." He drove off without another word.

Luke entered the house slowly with the keys he'd been given, unsure of what to expect. His relocation had taken a little longer than Sophia's and she would've likely felt isolated and lonely. His eyes scanned the small, neat interior. It appeared she'd taken the time to furnish and make it feel like a home. Wooden ceiling beams sloped downward on each side of the living space. Stacked firewood, almost up to the ceiling, framed the stone fireplace at the far end with a plush curved sofa in front. A fire had been lit, immediately warming his frozen cheeks and toes.

When his eyes finally landed on her standing by the small kitchen table, the shock of blonde hair startled him into silence. She resembled a Greek goddess only found in folklore.

She smiled as he continued to stare, her beauty radiating out, inviting him in. "I've been waiting for you," she finally said. Her deep sapphire eyes transformed to the color of clear blue Mediterranean Sea against her flaxen hair.

"I'm right here, Boss. Ready to serve."

Her smile turned into a wide grin as she launched herself toward him. His arms ached to crush her against him. Their tight embrace turned into a storm of kisses long overdue. All things left unsaid would take a backseat to previously restricted emotions, now unleashed.

But even after their moment of bliss, the gnawing reality came rushing back as Luke knew he had to tell her the truth about Tony. Even if she never forgave him for his death, keeping it from her would be infinitely worse.

He released her waist. "We should never speak of the past. We'll need to work on moving forward instead of thinking or talking about people we used to know. They will all soon be a distant memory. We should have no regrets about coming here. I want to build a new life with you and make an honest living. Whoever we meet from this day forward will know us as the Millers. They never need to know that you were running an illegal organization, and you never have to hear about who got whacked again. Does that sound good?"

She nodded. "I think I might need some time to adjust."

"Naturally." Luke took her hand and led her to the couch. As he sat next to her, his knee bounced incessantly. What he was about to say would change her forever. He considered keeping it to himself, but he knew he couldn't live a normal life with lies following him around like the grim reaper. Swallowing the massive lump in his throat, he forced his vocal cords to function. "I have something to tell you."

Her eyes opened wide. "Oh, no. What did you do? You didn't hurt anyone, did you?"

His eyebrows scrunched together. "No, not exactly."

She looked up at the ceiling. "Do you have to tell

me? I don't think I can take any more bad news."

"I do have to tell you. It's about the arrest. When the Feds came."

"I thought they were just going to arrest them. Did someone get hurt? It didn't go well?"

Luke shook his head. "No, it didn't."

"What do you mean?"

"The Feds came out of nowhere, bursting into Luigi's pizza shop with their guns pointed at everyone, screaming to get down on the ground."

She scrunched up her face. "Ugh, that seems so dramatic."

"Sammy, Tony, Kid and I were all present when they showed up, but Tony resisted."

She leaned forward. "He resisted? He resisted arrest?"

Luke nodded. "Tony refused to go willingly. He went for his gun."

"Oh, no." She covered her face with her hands. "Don't say it." Her back shook as she began to cry.

He held her as she wept. "Obviously, that wasn't supposed to happen, but he was deemed a threat—"

"A threat? Tony Russo was the least of their problems. He was family."

"They were all family, but to what end? Until someone goes to prison or is whacked by a rival group member? It seems like a setup for the inevitable."

She sniffed. "That's the life I knew. He didn't deserve to die."

"No, he didn't. I wish there was something I could've done to stop it, but the Feds didn't even hesitate once he reached in his jacket."

She gritted her teeth. "If I could get my hands on

them, they wouldn't have any fingers left to pull any more triggers."

He squeezed her arm to calm her down, never fully accepting of her violent tendencies—it would be something they would need to work on. "Whoa. Whoa. No one's pulling out fingers. I get that you're mad but there was nothing I could do. Believe me, I want him back too, more than anything. But we've got to move forward now. It'll be hard knowing we were given the chance to go free, but it was their choice to participate in organized crime."

"A chance to go free? You mean to be a rat? None of them would've wanted that even if they were given the opportunity, regardless." She breathed in, shaking her head in disbelief. "I need time to process all of this. Right at this moment, I don't know if I can move on."

Luke looked at her glassy, inflamed eyes. "I understand you need time. Do you regret leaving?"

Shaking her head, "No, of course not. You know I wasn't happy. I couldn't go anywhere without someone trying to kill me or control me. But I feel as if we escaped one prison just to be brought to another one."

"This isn't a prison. You're Claire Miller, a successful digital fashion editor living in a beautiful house with amazing views and a good-looking partner."

She managed a weak laugh. "That sounds pretty good actually."

"It'll take some time, but I promise you'll be happier here. Will you try to be strong?"

She nodded, pressing tissue to one corner of her eye. "I'll try."

He leaned to kiss her lips for reassurance. They only had each other. To fall apart now would not be acceptable. "You did a great job with the place."

"Thanks. I was pretty bored waiting for you." A fresh set of tears forced their way onto her cheeks.

The small talk only seemed to make things worse. It would be a while before Sophia was herself again and he would ride this wave with her—whatever it took. "I'm glad you waited for me. I feel bad that I have to leave again."

She looked up at him as he stood up from the couch. "What? Where are you going?"

He smirked, diffusing her fear. "Troy forgot to give me a coat. If you're sending someone to frigid weather, at least give them a coat. I'm going into town to get one. Do you want to come with me?"

"No, I don't want to have a breakdown in public—not that many people will see me around here."

Luke hesitated, not wanting to leave her in her current state. "Are you sure?"

"I'm sure. Go get that coat. I need a minute to process everything anyway." She managed a weak smile.

"Sophia, remember, we're in this together. I'm here with you."

She nodded.

He opened the front door, cringing as the icy breeze blew through his cotton shirt. This weather would take some getting used to. "I'll be back soon." He walked out and shut the door behind him.

On the way over from Nevada in the car with Troy, he'd noticed a small clothing store that appeared to carry coats. Preferring to drive the larger of the two vehicles they'd been given to get around, Luke jumped into the old green pickup truck.

As he headed toward town, he noticed there weren't

many people around to worry about recognizing them. They could easily find work online and maybe he could find extra work in a bike shop—that is, if there was one in town. Things would be fine. He relaxed his shoulders, feeling confident this was the right decision.

After parking close to the entrance, he opened the door and was startled by a chime sound as he walked inside. Sweaters and jackets lined the clothing racks with barely any room to move through them. The men's section was on the left side, while the women's was on the opposite side. He hoped the prices were low given his current lack of funds—he would need to rectify that issue as soon as possible, hopefully with legal work.

Searching through the line of brown and black leather jackets, he thought he might need something warmer. Across the store he could see a handful of women furiously moving through the racks at high speed. His side of the room was fairly empty as he scanned the goose-down coats. At the corner of his eye, he felt the unmistakable feeling of someone staring at him. Heat coursed through his body as his body prepared for flight or fight. He moved toward the exit not wanting to tempt fate and end up back in the slammer. Trying to be inconspicuous, he handled a few more jackets before lifting his eyes toward the culprit. His hands froze in place, mouth drying up into ash.

Kid.

Luke couldn't believe his eyes. Kid stood a few feet away, staring him down like a boxer about to go many rounds. How had he gotten out of prison? Perhaps a crooked cop was paid off by the crew to keep tabs on him and Sophia? Did the Feds not have enough evidence on Kid for a conviction to stick? He had no idea.

And how had Kid found their location? A mole within the FBI leaking information to the crew? Rocco's video warning flashed in his mind. He'd warned Luke for any misstep he'd be hunted down like a hawk hunts a rat. He was wrong to believe he could easily walk away from a crime family. Regardless, he knew Kid had not been sent to take action because everyone knew he would not win in a one-on-one fight with Luke, but rather he was sent as a reminder that the Costa Crew knew where to find them.

Luke rushed out of the store without a coat, trying to catch his breath as he raced to the truck. He would not tell Sophia about this encounter. If he did, she would never feel at peace. He, on the other hand, would likely be looking over his shoulder for the rest of his life, as he'd been given a clear message that even if he tried to exist on the right side of the law, he would always be considered the bad guy.

Rushing back to the truck, his cell phone buzzed in his pocket. He'd ignored it the first couple of times it rang while he had been in the store, anxious to get away from Kid. As he reached for his phone and placed his hand on the handle of the driver's seat door, he heard someone calling his name.

"Luke! Get away from the truck! Run!"

He recognized the screaming voice as Sophia's, but instead of waiting to confirm, he launched himself back from the truck, falling hard onto the concrete and knocking the breath out of him. He rolled out of the way, using another parked car as a shield as his truck exploded into a ball of fire.

Flaming embers and car parts landed around him as he checked if all his limbs were intact. Bystanders stood with their jaws open in horror. The sound of sirens pierced his ears—someone must've notified the police. Finally rising from the ground as the heat pressed on his skin, Luke couldn't believe what he'd dodged.

Through the heavy black smoke, Sophia came running toward him. She slammed into him in a tight embrace.

"I'm all right. I'm all right," he reassured her.

"I tried calling to warn you, but you didn't pick up, so I drove here as fast as I could," she said breathlessly.

"How did you know?"

"As soon as you pulled out of the driveway, I noticed a dark blue SUV trailing you to town. With so few people around us, I thought it looked suspicious. It seemed like a long shot, but I thought it looked like Kid's SUV."

He kissed the top of her head. "It's probably someone with the same car." He looked around at the scene. "I don't see the SUV anywhere."

"Then who planted the bomb? Earl from the flower shop?" Sarcasm oozed from her lips. "You don't have to protect me from the mobsters. I am one of them, remember?"

"You *were* one of them and we're smarter than them as long as we stick together."

"Let's go home. The authorities will handle it."

"And probably get nowhere on it," he replied.

She nodded. "That's correct. See, you learned something as a member of the Costa Crew. If they wanted to kill us, we would already be dead. This is a scare tactic to potentially continue for the rest of our lives."

"You would know, you are the boss."

She smiled.

"You're smiling even though my truck was just blown up seconds before I got into it?"

"I'm not happy about *that*. You know what I am pleased about?"

Luke couldn't imagine a single positive thing about this but that was Sophia, always surprising him and never playing the victim.

"I'm pleased that for once I saved you this time."

Chapter Twenty-Two

Sophia bolted upright in bed, sweat dripping down the front of her T-shirt. Night after night at three o'clock in the morning, her mind would replay the scene of Luke narrowly losing his life to the car bombing, sending her into a tailspin. Fueled by anxiety, her mind raced with scenarios of what might happen to them next. The Costa Crew would not go down quietly and from what she'd learned growing up around them, torturing others was as easy to them as putting cream cheese on a bagel.

On top of that, if they had cooperation from authorities who were paid off or coerced, it would be even easier. However, living in fear had not been how she wanted to spend the rest of her life and exposing Luke to her unease would not be helpful in moving forward with their relationship.

And so, she hid her fears from him until the day a strange car pulled up in their driveway. Sophia kept her gun ready to defend her new life.

"That's Troy's car," Luke said, sliding the kitchen curtain away. "You can relax, put the gun down. He's probably checking in on us after what happened with the truck."

But Sophia had no intention of relaxing her stance. Her experience in the mafia had taught her to trust no one and to never let her guard down. The one exception to that rule was how she'd behaved when she met Luke—

for that she had no regrets.

She decided to be cautious and stay out of view as she watched Luke open the door and casually let Troy walk in, carrying a basket of baked goods.

"Are we in trouble?" Luke joked. "Have you come to arrest us?"

"No, I already did that, remember?" Troy walked in, handing the basket to Luke.

"Thanks. That's mighty nice of you. These corn muffins look familiar."

"I got them from our favorite spot, Desert Oasis Diner. I figured you must miss meeting me there time after time."

Luke laughed. "Right, I can't say that I do, but thanks for bringing them." He led Troy inside to the small round kitchen table. He grabbed three of the muffins from the basket and set them on the table where a coffee carafe had been placed earlier.

"I love what you've done with the place," Troy said, pulling a chair out to sit.

"I had no part in that," Luke said. "It was all Sophia's doing."

"How's it going for you two?" Troy asked.

Luke cocked his head to one side. "Not bad, it's a bit isolating out here but we're keeping busy. Sophia's been working online. She seems to be enjoying her job. We joke that maybe someday she'll be the boss since that's what she's accustomed to. I found a job fixing up motorcycles and ATVs at an auto repair shop. The owner, Jacob, lets me pick the jobs I want to take on for the most part. I've also been applying to computer schools online since I never got to pursue that growing up."

Troy smiled. "Not bad for an ex-con and an ex-mob boss."

"We're trying to take advantage of our time, so that's been good, except for the car bombing incident, which I'm sure you heard about."

Troy nodded. "I heard about it. You're very lucky to come out of that in one piece."

"My bodyguard, Sophia, who has a lot of experience with that type of threat, warned me before the car exploded. It was likely Costa Crew retaliation, wouldn't you agree?"

"I wouldn't put it past them. It's the type of gruesome tactic the mafia tends to employ. There's no doubt someone wants you dead."

"But how would they know where to find me?"

"Maybe they had someone follow my car when we drove here, and I dropped you off. It's not the first time I've seen that happen. We can try to relocate you, but I fear they probably have eyes on you wherever you go. We'd have to kidnap you in the middle of the night and fly you two somewhere in a private plane overseas to really throw them off."

"That's insane and not very reassuring."

"I never said it was going to be a spa retreat here. You definitely need to watch your back until we have a good plan in place for relocation. It's also very costly and needs approval."

Sophia watched as Troy schmoozed with Luke. The hairs on the back of her neck stood up the minute Luke spotted his car in the driveway. She couldn't explain it but something about him bothered her. She blamed him for Tony's death. Even though Luke had explained that Troy had not been the one who fired at Tony during the arrest, she felt that he was responsible for what went down that day. She argued he hadn't tried hard enough to keep everyone safe that day. He failed Luke and he failed Tony. For him to come over now to check in on them after the car bomb seemed a little too late for redemption. Luke had never really spent as much time as she had dealing with the way mobsters think. Maybe she was wrong about Troy, but she was going to listen to her gut and her gut was telling her to watch him closely.

Tucking the gun in the waistband of her jeans behind her back, she made her way into the kitchen. "Did you frisk him? One can never be too safe these days," she said, pouring coffee into mugs.

"Ah, good morning, Sophia. I can assure you as a federal agent, I am packing heat," Troy said with his hands up. "Dare I say, I love the blonde hair. It's like you're a completely different person—at least, on the outside."

She smirked in reply.

"No, I didn't frisk him," Luke said with sarcasm. "He brought muffins."

"Oh, good. Maybe they're poisoned," she said.

"Oh, come on," Luke said. "Not everyone is trying to murder us."

"Can't be too sure," Sophia said.

Troy grabbed one of the muffins and stared at her as he took a large bite out of it, chewing aggressively and swallowing it down with the coffee she'd poured.

"Now that we settled that issue, on to the next one," Sophia said. "We want answers."

"Geez, Sophia. The man just got here," Luke said.

Troy put his free hand up to stop him. "She's right. That's why I'm here." He put the coffee mug down. "I

190

feel terrible about what happened to Tony. That was not part of the plan."

"Obviously it wasn't part of the plan," Sophia said, seething with anger. "Couldn't you have done a better job to prevent it?"

He shook his head. "There was nothing we could've done differently. Tony reached for his gun—that's a big no-no when federal agents have guns pointed at your face yelling at you to get on the ground."

Sophia sat back on her heels, eyes wide. "A big no-no?" Then she leaned forward pointing her finger at Troy. "I'll tell you what's a big *no-no*, killing my friends."

Troy stared at her, visibly annoyed. "I came here as a courtesy to see how things were going and if there's anything I can do for you. Luke left quite an impression on me during his time as an informant. We don't usually drop by with baked goods, but I respect Luke for his skills and dedication to the mission."

"Oh." Sophia's voice rose. "How thoughtful. Were you coming by to make sure Luke's skin hadn't melted off when his car exploded?"

Luke lifted his hand to calm her. "Sophia, it's all right."

"Sort of, yeah," Troy replied. "I heard about it and—"

"And what?" Sophia taunted him. "You wanted to come here and tell us how that wasn't supposed to happen? That the car blowing up a second before Luke got in it wasn't part of the plan?"

Troy stared at her stone-faced. "Well, on the contrary, it was part of the plan."

She stood with her hands on her hips, stunned. Then

she leaned forward. "I'm sorry?"

"Luke can attest to the fact that I've made it my personal mission to wipe out the mafia organization ever since one of them took out my partner in a shootout." His eyes grew colder by the second. "I've seen a lot of criminals in my time, but your people are by far the worst."

"Everyone needs a hobby, I suppose," Sophia said, dismissing his speech. "You'll never succeed. The organization has networks that no one can penetrate, not even the FBI."

"Troy, *we* are not part of the organization," Luke interjected. "*You* brought me in it, and Sophia has always wanted to leave the organization. We are not the same as them."

"Ah"—Troy lifted his pointer finger—"I thought Luke was my golden boy. He'd been so successful in infiltrating the Costa Crew, I even considered sending him for other missions. Until he started telling me how he'd become friends with the enemy and that he couldn't tell which side he was on."

"It was confusing at the time. You said you understood," Luke said.

"Even if I let that go," Troy said, "you wanted to bring the boss of the Costa Crew with you. Of all things." Troy lifted his hands up in disbelief.

"So, what are you saying?" Luke asked. "Are you the mole? Did you get Kid out of prison to torment us?"

Sophia stared in Luke's direction. He'd been keeping things from her.

"You had Kid plant a car bomb?" Sophia asked, putting two and two together.

Troy shrugged. "Why not use him? The Costa Crew

is pretty pissed off at you for faking your way to the top and getting them arrested. You toyed with their emotions." He tapped his chest. "I'd be pretty pissed off, too."

Anger coursed through her veins, making her hands shake. The same man who had helped Luke and her escape the mafia had turned on them for some personal vendetta.

"And you've come here to pretend you're looking out for us when you are actually trying to control us?" Luke asked rhetorically. "To get us to do your dirty work against the Costa Crew?"

"I could be convinced not to consider you two as part of the problem if certain promises could be kept," Troy said. "As you can see, the players in this game change quite often."

Sophia kept her hands behind her back. They were shaking uncontrollably but she knew it was now or never. Troy had broken her heart once by allowing Tony to get shot and he almost succeeded in doing it again by attempting to murder Luke. She would not survive that. Troy had to go.

Yanking the gun from her waist, she pointed it at Troy. "Does this seem convincing?"

Troy put his hands up. "Aw, come on, Sophia. We can all try to work together. Luke and I have an undeniable history together. He has more talent than some of the agents on the force, and you never liked where you came from. We can move past it all and start fresh."

"I don't think so, Troy. I think you'll be plucking away at us one at a time. We can never trust you."

"Come on, Luke. You were never a fan of violence.

Where's that guy who never wanted to see anyone get killed?"

"I'm still that guy, but I think I'm going to let Sophia handle this one."

Troy backed up a bit, looking around, clearly searching for an escape.

"She's the one you hadn't thought much about in this plan. Am I right?" Luke said. "She's the one who should not be underestimated."

"She was controlled by the other members and Rocco," Tony said. "You were the one who kept telling me she wasn't one of them, remember?"

"I have been underestimated," Sophia said. "Maybe I do want a different life, but I was certainly raised in it, and I learned a lot. You don't think that I can't make this look like an accident?" she taunted. "You don't think we can make you disappear into thin air?"

Troy swallowed hard. "I don't think you realize what happens when you cause any kind of bodily harm to a federal agent. The repercussions will ruin your new fabulous lives as Claire and Tom Miller."

"I'll take my chances," she said, gripping the gun harder.

Troy smiled eerily. "You might be able to make me disappear, Sophia, and maybe no one will care, but what about those teenagers?"

Her eyes shifted to Luke, not wanting him to hear more.

"Oh, he already knows about poor Carla and Matteo because I told him."

Her breathing became more rapid as fury took over.

"We can give you a new name, Sophia, and you can run from your old self, but you will always be the cold, calculating killer that ended two innocent children's lives."

She shook her head. "They were not innocent children. They had grown up on the street, stealing, pillaging, and murdering."

Troy took a step forward, presumably trying to regain control of the scene.

"I wouldn't test her, Troy. She's not like me," Luke warned.

But Troy continued to slowly creep forward, like an alligator waiting for its moment to pounce. "I wonder how Luke feels about living under the same roof as a murderer?"

She gritted her teeth. "It takes one to know one."

Troy stopped inching forward but instead lunged at her, trying to grab the gun.

Adrenaline burst through Sophia's veins as her fingers reacted, pulling the trigger before he could grab her gun.

He crumpled to the ground, holding his chest, eyes wide. His breathing became labored. "I wasn't expecting that from you."

"That's what happens when you underestimate me," she answered, her arms shaking as she kept her gun aimed at him.

"I should've known. You are a mobster." He took a few more breaths, then succumbed to his wounds.

"I should've seen this coming," Luke said. "He told me he wanted to eradicate the mafia, but I didn't think that meant we were also part of his plans. He probably planned all along to shoot us and I let him in the door."

"Don't blame yourself. There's no way you would've known. The fact that he allowed me to come with you into witness protection was not normal practice. But he had done that to please you. He'd been planning to use you as his mafia member eradicator but hadn't expected you to actually like it."

"I wouldn't say I liked it. I like you, even though you have violent tendencies."

She didn't smile. "It came in handy this time."

"Troy Wilson was the last person I thought would be considered the bad guy in all of this," Luke said.

"Troy isn't the bad guy," she said. "Neither are you. I'm the bad guy."

A word about the author…

When Ana Diamond isn't writing about tough gals finding love in unexpected places, she's at work by day in the medical field. She writes romantic mystery novels with feisty strong women and alluring men who can't resist them. Her books are fast paced, entertaining and heartfelt all at once.

Ana is a 2020 Tara Contest Finalist for Body Conscious and 2015 Melody of Love contest finalist. She lives in New York with her husband and two children.

http://anadiamondauthor.com

Thank you for purchasing
this publication of The Wild Rose Press, Inc.

For questions or more information
contact us at
info@thewildrosepress.com.

The Wild Rose Press, Inc.
www.thewildrosepress.com